Dust

Adrián Bravi

DUST

Translated from the Italian by Patience Haggin

DALKEY ARCHIVE PRESS

Originally published in Italian by Nottetempo as *La pelusa* in 2007.

First Dalkey Archive edition, 2017.

Library of Congress Cataloging-in-Publication Data
Names: Bravi, Adrián N., 1963- author. | Haggin, Patience, translator.
Title: Dust / Adrián N. Bravi ; translated by Patience Haggin.
Other titles: Pelusa. English
Description: First Dalkey archive edition. | Victoria, TX : Dalkey Archive edition, 2017. | "Originally published in Italian by Edizioni Nottetempo as La Pelusa in 2007" -- Verso title page. | Includes bibliographical references and index.
Identifiers: LCCN 2017035400 | ISBN 9781943150335 (pbk. : alk. paper)
Subjects: LCSH: Librarians--Fiction. | Dust--Fiction. | Regression (Civilization)--Fiction. | Phobias--Fiction. | Obsessive-compulsive disorder--Fiction. | Psychological fiction.
Classification: LCC PQ4902.R388 P4613 2017 | DDC 853/.92--dc23
LC record available at https://lccn.loc.gov/2017035400

The translation of this book was made possible by support from the Italian Ministry of Foreign Affairs and International Cooperation.

Questo libro è stato tradotto grazie ad un contributo alla traduzione assegnato dal Ministero degli Affari Esteri e della Cooperazione Internazionale Italiano.

www.dalkeyarchive.com
Victoria, TX / McLean, IL / Dublin

Dalkey Archive Press publications are, in part, made possible through the support of the University of Houston-Victoria and its programs in creative writing, publishing, and translation.

Printed on permanent/durable acid-free paper

Translator's Preface

Dust is titled *La pelusa*, after the Spanish word that Anselmo learns from the author's eponymous character to describe dust.

Yet *Dust* is not a book about dust. Rather, it is a book about books. Its protagonist looks for meaning and identity in books, whether he is chasing his own intellectual whims or believing he knows his mysterious Argentine acquaintance through his reading. Homages to the Italian poet Giacomo Leopardi (1798-1837) pervade the novel. Anselmo is described as a man who "sees the infinite in everything," in an allusion to Leopardi's most famous poem, "L'infinito." He lives in the fictional city of Catinari, a near-anagram of Leopardi's home city, Recanati, where the author himself dwells. The book includes still more allusions to other writers from Leopardi's time. For example, Anselmo's mysterious book about old books is written by an author named Baldacchini, an allusion to a contemporary of Leopardi's by that name. Bravi's eponymous character requests books by naturalist William Henry Hudson, and is familiar with the work of English essayist John Wilkins.

Anselmo, named after the Catholic saint who founded Scholastic thought, brings religious devotion and a penchant for philosophical inquiry to both his career as a librarian and his struggle to keep his home clean. His last name, Del Vescovo, means bishop, in an allusion to Saint Anselm's time as the archbishop of Canterbury. In one undeliverable message to his friend Paolo, Anselmo echoes the line from Genesis: "dust thou art, and unto dust shalt thou return."

In translating Bravi, I have taken care to preserve the precision and obsession with classification that define this novel's style. I have taken care to preserve also the military allegories that Bravi, a veteran of the Falklands War, invokes as Anselmo defends his home from siege. In translating Bravi's beautiful, imaginative descriptions of dust's swirling menace, I have taken care to maintain the consistency of certain key phrases that recur throughout the novel.

I owe an enormous debt to Dalkey Archive Press publisher John O'Brien for championing the novel and advising me throughout the long process of completing this translation. I am indebted also to Dalkey's Nathan Redman for copyediting this translation and Jake Snyder for helping me navigate the process. I'm very grateful as well to Maria Leonardi at Edizioni Nottetempo, who was very supportive of bringing this fascinating novel into English. And I could not have translated this book, nor ever aspired to the great privilege of knowing the Italian language and culture, without the lifelong support of my family.

Mr. Bravi loved and cared for this poignant novel so much that he even inserted himself into the text. I salute Mr. Bravi for his passion, and hope that I have given his fascinating novel the English version it deserves.

"Of the individual parts composing the human body, some are fluid, some soft, some hard."

Spinoza, *Ethics* (Part II, Postulate II)

Part I

Anselmo awoke with the first trill of his alarm that morning, just as he did every morning. He rubbed his eyes and put on his glasses, then watched his bedroom furniture come into focus: the lamp hanging from the ceiling, his coat on its stand. He got up and made his bed, just as he always did. A light so dim it was nearly undetectable seeped through the shutters. The garbage collectors were already out in the street. He walked down the hall, still in his pajamas, then stopped in front of the window and stretched. On the kitchen table was a magazine his wife had been reading before bed. He opened it to a random page and read in blaring letters: LUKEWARM, HOT, OR SCALDING: WHAT'S YOUR SEX SCORE? He unscrewed the filter from the espresso maker, sat back down, propped his elbows on the table, and stared straight ahead. Outside the streetlamps were still lit and the town was quiet, just as it always was on cold mornings.

Anselmo finished his coffee, got up from the table, and started cleaning the house. He remembered something his wife told him she'd read recently: that people who obsess over a clean home had suffered some traumatic experience of fear or abandonment at some point in their lives, though they may not know exactly when. They have an obsessive desire to return to the sterile walls of their mother's womb, his wife said, and see home as a shelter from the corrupted world. They see filth and disorder as intruders bringing chaos into their sacred refuge, she said. And sometimes, Elena went on, people even go mad from believing the entire world is contaminated.

"Why should I care? If someone thinks I'm a lunatic because I notice the drizzle of dust that forms on every surface overnight, what's it to me?" Anselmo thought as he squeezed a few drops of cleanser onto a wet rag and bent down to clear off the dust that had stirred and then settled down again after his first pass at the table. "People who write those magazine articles can think whatever they want. I don't care. I don't go around criticizing what other people do. If I want to wipe away some dust, I get a rag and do it. So what if that means I'm trying to clean the walls of my mother's womb?"

He went back into his study and opened a window that looked out on a view of colorful old roofs set against a phalanx of poppies. He leaned over the desk and saw a thin, almost imperceptible layer of dust covering the phone, notebooks, and lamp. "Cleaning is never finished!" he said, grimacing. He glanced at his watch, annoyed. He didn't have much time, but before anything else he had to get rid of this new topsoil that had settled everywhere. But now that the natural light was stronger, he could see that the tabletop was even dirtier, which made him furious. He shut the window and turned off the lamp. It was no small task fighting the grime that invaded his home every night and conquered all his possessions. But afterward he felt relieved. Rubbing away the filth, seeing it disappear with his own eyes, calmed him. Finally he turned on the tap in the bathroom, waited until the water grew hot, then rinsed out the cloth, just as he did every day.

Anselmo was someone who saw the infinite in everything, down to the slightest detail. But he always saw it as tiny particles floating through the air looking for the best place to settle. This was how he liked to imagine the degradation that crept into his home, as a shapeless debris continually eroding and disintegrating. In Anselmo's eyes, dust itself wasn't fire, or air, or earth, or water—yet all of these had dust in them. Dust was in the light of fire, when he opened the window and a sunbeam laid bare to his horrified eyes the chaotic swarm of crazed particles celebrating the light's presence. Dust was in the air when he swept cobwebs from the corners of the ceiling. Dust was in the earth when the rains stopped and the wind did its work of spreading dust throughout the world. And there was even dust in water, as it swirled all those microscopic beings together and ferried them to the sewers. Under his floor lay a network of small pipes, which connected to larger pipes for the whole building and eventually connected with huge pipes that ran beneath the entire city and took the dust who knows where, along with hair, germs, microbes, feces, and all the world's refuse. But knowing that somehow water dragged all this filth far away set his heart at peace. He couldn't see dust as any of the four elements—not the beauty of fire, or the lightness of air, or the solidity of earth, and absolutely not the vitality of water—but he knew that it was present in all of them, inside and outside every single thing. "Dust is everywhere," he thought. "Even in heaven there will be dust."

After he cleaned the study, he opened the window and closed the door behind him. He looked at the clock and saw he still had time. He went into the bathroom and turned on the shower, letting it flow into the basin. And just as he often did, he went onto the balcony off his bedroom where he was sure no one could see him. He took off his night jacket, then his wool sweater—but very slowly, since wool, being a great magnet for dust, was one of the fabrics that tormented him most.

He took off his pajamas and undershirt. He plucked some hairs from his chest, the weak ones that came off on their own, and threw them down onto the street. Finally he took off his slippers, socks, pants, and underwear. He picked them up one at a time and shook them out over the balcony. He liked watching the wind carry that cloud of dust away from his home. He tossed his clothes in the hamper and came back inside, shivering. Feeling that he'd finished something, he got into the shower.

"If I had it my way, I'd live my whole life under a stream of water," he thought. He dried himself off and went to get clean clothes out of his closet. By now he felt ready for work. Remembering what his wife had said about the womb made him think that someone could surely clean his house thoroughly without going mad from it. "Only a nut could call someone a nut just for cleaning his home," he thought, almost indignant.

"Are you leaving?" his wife asked from the bed, where she lay curled up under the comforter.

"Yes," answered Anselmo, adjusting his tie in the mirror.

"Are you coming home for lunch?"

"I don't know."

He walked to the bed, where his wife pulled her arms out from under the comforter and looked at him drowsily. He was about to kiss her, until he smelled her repulsive, vodka-soaked breath.

"I left the window open in the study, so remember to close it when you get up. Actually, close it after you have breakfast. The study needs to be aired out."

"I'll just close it on my way out."

"No, no, that's too late. There's a dry wind out there and I don't want it to fill the house up with dust all over again. And don't forget the bedroom windows too," he added from the hallway.

He put on his hat and left. With a grimace he took in his first breath of fresh air. He hurried to the bus stop, then waited, checking his watch.

"Whenever I'm on time, the bus is late," he thought, tapping on his watch impatiently. Like all anxious people, he cared about punctuality. He took a few steps back so he wouldn't have to suffer the rush of cars blowing tiny particles of dust onto his head. Sometimes he thought cars came by just for this purpose, just to taunt him. The trucks, vans, buses, and everything else that rumbled down that street raised up smells from the sewers, which combined with the filth that every night left on the pavement and made him sick to his stomach. He never felt safe from it, no matter how much he washed his hands and face. It was stronger than him. There was nothing he could do but tolerate the presence of these microscopic beings that flitted through the air. And even if he managed to keep dust in check within his home by cleaning every day, it was impossible everywhere else. He kept away from certain places, avoided certain streets, protected his head with a hat, and stayed far from strangers who might transmit their dust to him. Each article of clothing he put on gave him more armor against the infinite particles charging at him every moment.

Anselmo was a tall man of few words. He had the slightest of twitches in his eye. No one noticed it except his wife, who saw it as a sign of exhaustion rather than an involuntary nervous impulse. He worked full time at the Catinari Public Library, and, even though there wasn't much to do in the Catinari Public Library, performed his duties more diligently than any of his colleagues, never wasting a moment or showing a sign of frustration. But if there were any issue to be resolved, he dedicated himself to solving it, even if it meant staying late. He worked without caring about his coworkers' gossip or the way they looked him over, head to toe, when he arrived and stamped his time card. Still, he was conscious of having to work with two parasites, and occasionally felt stranded in the middle of a sea. He never spoke to them beyond a simple greeting and whatever short exchanges the job demanded. It wasn't that his colleagues had ever done anything in particular to offend him. Rather, he simply wanted to keep his distance, as he considered them the victims of two evil forces: sloth and indigestion. Both suffered from constipation, judging from how frequently they spoke of it, along with depression, menstrual cramps, migraines, and more. They'd tried more than once to drag him into their dull conversations, but hit a brick wall every time, since Anselmo would stiffen up and refuse to answer. And if they asked him what he'd done that weekend he answered, "Just the usual." He never revealed anything, and not just because it was rare for him to do anything worth telling. To them he seemed ethereal, unmoored from the facts of reality. Still, notwithstanding Anselmo's aversion to conversation, his colleagues knew a few things about him: that he'd been married for two years, that he lived in an apartment he inherited from his parents, that for some reason he didn't want children, that he preferred to take the bus rather than drive a car, that he always wore a hat to protect himself from the wind. But they knew nothing of his dust phobia. Anselmo let out all that frustration at home, as a rule. Outside his home he tolerated dust, he'd resigned himself to it. He had no means of fighting it. He confined his struggle to the walls of his home, to the walls of the womb that he could never clean as much as he wanted. Besides that, people had never been his strong suit, and his coworkers were no exception.

One of his coworkers was a fifty-year-old woman with a pesky lisp in her teeth and an odd habit of never looking him in the eye when she spoke to him. She always aimed her gaze slightly above, as if she were addressing someone perched on his head. Her conversation was always the same: her savings, money transfers, new retirement policies, trips she did or didn't want to take. Every day she stamped her time card and waited impatiently until she could go home. His other coworker was forty-five and had a nervous look, with a large forehead (ironic given her tiny brain, Anselmo thought) and traces of a dark mustache above her lips. She'd been hired in the library after being injured by the mayor's horse, though she never discussed this. As much as the mayor's horse supposedly loved giving rides, it had broken two fingers on this woman's right hand. And to make amends the mayor had done his best to set her up with a job in the library, where having two broken fingers wouldn't compromise her work, since she could still sort books with one hand. With time Anselmo had begun to think of his two coworkers as a single being, always resting its four hands and four buttocks on the radiator. When either one was alone, she became nicer and more efficient, as if she felt obliged to make a bit more of an effort. When they were together they instinctively turned lazy. Anselmo imagined that life typically passed by in a blur for each of them, then slowed down a bit when they were together. In his mind he called them the "lazy ladies."

That day the bus came late and Anselmo had to stamp his time card twelve minutes late, which was exasperating. "I run, I do all I can to be on time, and then, because of some crazy distracted bus driver, I'm late anyway." He took off his coat and sat down to work. He had plenty to do and didn't like to leave with things unfinished. He didn't mind working through lunch. It gave him time to read something or resolve the cataloging issues that could be such a headache. But that day, after he'd organized all he could, he spent lunch in the office reading a chapter on the myth of Aristaeus. Then he returned to cataloging in the afternoon.

He was cataloging a training manual for financial advisors when he raised his eyes from his screen and saw the older of the lazy ladies. She stood staring out the window, leaning her hands on the radiator, as usual. She looked sad, as if she were fed up with waiting sixty years to retire. Four years earlier she'd been transferred from the city tax office, where there was nothing to do, to the library, and where she'd somehow done less than nothing. Some directors had thought she'd be more suited to library work and transferred her there, where she could attach herself to the radiator every day until she hit sixty, and no one would notice that she did less than nothing. Anselmo watched her looking over his computer screen, then looked down at the title page of the training manual. A thought popped into his head: "How can you work in a library when you've never even seen an old book? When you can't tell paper from parchment? When you don't even know how Gutenberg's printing press worked?" He looked at his coworker and then down at the training manual, but his mind was filled with medieval manuscripts, with their paper, watermarks, movable type . . . He instantly felt plunged into a deep lacuna between two worlds. In the whole time he'd been working at the Catinari Public Library he'd never handled an old book. In fact, he'd never in his life held a fifty-year-old book, much less a medieval one. He considered himself a warehouseman who specialized in books, nothing more. He cataloged them, put them on the shelves, and decided which bestsellers to buy next season. "How can I be a librarian when I've never even held a fifty-year-old book?" he thought, watching his coworker yearn for retirement. While the Catinari Public Library had no rule against it, he was certain that its dreary regular patrons had never taken interest in an old book, much less asked any of the librarians for one. He absolutely had to confront this problem sooner or later, and he wondered only how. He called a bookseller outside the city and asked if they had any old books available. The bookseller made a quick search and then gave two names: Baldacchini and Zappella. Anselmo chose Baldacchini, for no particular reason. When he left for the day, he took the bus directly to the bookstore.

"Here it is," said the bookseller, handing him the Baldacchini. Anselmo took a peek at the index, where he glimpsed enchanting antique frontispieces and a hunting scene taken from Giovanni Pietro Olina's *Uccelliera*.

When he arrived home, later than usual, he found his wife a bit lost in thought.

"I went to a bookstore outside of town to get this," Anselmo said, showing her the Baldacchini. He took off his shoes on the doorstep and put on his slippers. "You don't think you can be a good librarian without ever touching an old book, do you?"

"Of course not. That would be like studying smoke your whole life when you've never even seen fire," his wife answered. She took his shoes into the spare bathroom to clean them.

Anselmo watched her, thinking. He decided her analogy to smoke was exactly right.

"That's why," he said, stepping over the threshold in his slippers, "you always have to start from the beginning. We're getting too used to doing everything backward. Before I forget, how long was the bedroom window open?"

"About twenty minutes," his wife answered from the bathroom, where she was scrubbing his shoes vigorously.

"Twenty minutes? . . . Maybe you should've left it open for another ten."

"In this cold? I turned on the radiators an hour ago."

"Let's open it for another three or four minutes, just enough to clean the air a bit. It's so humid outside, there's no risk of dust getting in."

His wife went into the bedroom and opened the window. Dinner was ready, the table was set. Anselmo shook out his clothes on the balcony, took a quick shower and then sat at the table. He drank a glass of water and then began to eat the saffron rice his wife had prepared. Then he paused, pointed to the still-steaming plate, and said, "I think a bit of Parmesan wouldn't hurt, what do you think?"

"Why not?"

He got up to get the cheese, since his wife hadn't set it out on the table. Before he opened the refrigerator he saw that a very thin layer of dust had settled on its white metal door. He stood stock-still and studied it, running the tip of his index finger along the surface. His finger left a streak through the dust. He sat back down, grated some cheese for himself, and resumed eating. But he was agitated. He couldn't focus his attention on the plate of saffron rice. He couldn't stop thinking about the dust on the refrigerator and all the things it could harbor: dead insects, flakes of skin, dried soap, hair, fibers of thread, plaster from the walls, sand from far-off lands, and countless other disgusting materials. He could no longer eat. He went back to the refrigerator and ran his cloth over it once, then again and again. Elena stopped eating as well, filled with guilt for not noticing it first. She apologized to her husband as he rinsed out the cloth in the spare bathroom.

"I'll have to pay more attention," she thought, though she knew her eyes would never be as vigilant as Anselmo's.

"Again, I'm so sorry. I didn't notice . . ." she said.

"I know," he whispered, irritated.

Elena came back to the table and resumed eating, her cheeks stained pink. She didn't say a word for the rest of the meal. When they finished, she went to the kitchen window, where, by the light of the streetlamps, she could see a short ways down the street. For a moment she thought happily of her childhood in the country, how she used to watch the road through a window as she drifted off to sleep in front of the warm wood fire that lit her every memory from this time. She remembered cucumbers soaked in garlic and parsley brine, and her dogs barking at the passing cars.

Then she started to clear the table. All this time Anselmo had leaned against the radiator, waiting. When she was finished, Anselmo picked up the tablecloth and brought its four corners together, gathering the breadcrumbs, mandarin seeds, and other remnants of dinner. He went out on the balcony off the kitchen, made sure no one was looking, then unfolded the tablecloth and let the crumbs fall into the building courtyard. He shook the cloth out hard and went back into the kitchen. He usually did all this himself, since he couldn't bear to watch his wife pick up the tablecloth without bringing all four corners together. So he waited while his wife cleared the table and then took it upon himself to handle the tablecloth and save the floor from any possible debris, even if he would've cleaned it up the next day in any case. When it came to cleaning, there were some techniques that Elena just couldn't understand. Sometimes she expressly asked her husband how to clean something—for example, the shelves in the cabinet, where she kept the little wooden animals she'd bought from the Senegalese artisans. Anselmo had showed her, brusquely, how to clean them without stirring up dust. He knew he would have to do it himself anyway, since she would've forgotten everything by the next day. On the other hand, he hated wasting so many words explaining something he found so elementary, something his wife should've understood immediately. In effect, Anselmo wanted her to understand everything naturally, without explanation, about the war he waged against the world around him, against absolutely nothing, and how it tormented him day and night.

After dinner he went into his room and began reading the Baldacchini. At first he wanted to devour it in one gulp, as he did when a book was important. He took notes in a notebook. He stopped at every footnote. He even wanted to find every text Baldacchini cited and get a solid understanding of those books. But after the first chapter, his initial zeal began to flag. He skipped some footnotes that earlier he would've studied, and his eyelids began to feel terribly heavy. Then he scolded himself for not starting with the third chapter, for it looked the most interesting. The third chapter discussed an old book's visual elements: the letters, the frontispiece, the typography, etc. He looked at his watch. Now it was too late to wade into that argument. He went to bed, leaving the third chapter for the next day.

The alarm rang at exactly six the next morning. Anselmo lingered in bed, trying to reconstruct the dream he'd been having. Yet he remembered nothing but a few meaningless images. Then Elena began mumbling words under her breath, trying to resist some awful horror in her sleep. Her legs quivered nervously, as if trying to break free of a heavy chain around her ankles. Anselmo watched her, puzzled, and wondered what she could be dreaming. He wondered if it was caused by the saffron rice, or the vodka they drank before bed. Either way, he didn't care. It disgusted him to think that Elena's every kick under the sheets sent a gust of air across the bed, and that gust of air brought with it a repugnant menagerie of winged microbes, skin flakes, and tiny beings that would spawn between the hairs on his chest without him even noticing it. For a moment he imagined those horrendous beasts clinging to his body, building nests between his pinky and ring finger, behind his ears or on the back of his thigh. He even imagined that a flock of these winged microbes followed every gust of air that rose up when his wife moved her legs. He wanted to shout and wake her up, just so he could keep her still. He didn't do that. At first he tried to hold her feet still with his, but then Elena only thrashed about more violently, fighting to free herself from two grips: her nightmare and her husband. The sheets and the comforter rose and fell, sending old, stagnant air over the bed. There was no way to stop her. Anselmo didn't want to get under the covers, where he thought there must be an entire kingdom of mites by now. But he gathered his courage. He reached down and grabbed his wife's legs with all his might, so he could stop whatever was stirring up and fluttering about everywhere. She kneed him in the chin, which made him lose his grip for a moment. When he grabbed her legs again, she cried out, frantic. She woke up with her heart in her throat and saw her husband under the covers, holding back her legs.

"What the hell were you dreaming?" Anselmo asked, coming out from under the sheets.

"Nothing," Elena answered, putting her hand to her still-heaving chest.

"What kind of nothing?"

"Nothing."

"You made quite a mess."

"I'm sorry."

"Look at the sheets. They're everywhere."

"I'll fix them."

"And the microbes? What'll you do about the microbes?"

"What microbes?"

"Don't pretend you don't know."

"What?"

"Elena, do you realize how many microbes are flying around this room thanks to your feet?"

"I'm sorry. I'll fix it."

"I'll fix it, I'll fix it . . . Do you know how many times I've heard you say you'll fix everything, and then you don't?"

"I swear, I'll get every microbe."

"You don't even know where they are."

"Didn't you say they were in the room?"

"Yes, but do you know how to get them?"

"Well, tell me how."

"Do you see? If I didn't tell you the microbes were all over the room, you wouldn't have even noticed. You would've just gotten up. You wouldn't have even opened the window. You must be crazy. How can you not notice the cesspool you unleashed?"

"Just tell me what to do, and I'll do it."

"We can't live like this."

"Do you want me to spray the insecticide?"

"See? You don't understand at all. How would insecticide help? You'd kill them and then all their dried out bodies would still be lying here, and our bed would be a huge battlefield full of dead things. That's what you'd do. It's not about killing them. The point is they shouldn't be here at all, alive or dead. Don't you understand?"

"Yes, of course."

"No, I don't think you understand anything at all. Stay right there, I'll fix it myself."

Anselmo got up from the bed and headed for the bathroom. He rinsed off his face. As he squeezed the toothpaste tube he imagined the revolting jungle he would live in, if he became a microbe that lived its life trapped between the fibers of a broom. And he stood there, with the toothpaste in one hand and the toothbrush in the other, lost in thought as he tried to imagine the world where those ghastly little things lived. The toothpaste eked out steadily, in a cylinder swirl of the most beautiful colors. He raised his thumb, and the tube sucked one or two centimeters' worth of toothpaste back inside.

He made a coffee and, while he waited for the water to boil in the pot, put his hands near the blue-tipped flame, which at that hour of the day was at its most beautiful. Then he turned, looked at the white surface of the refrigerator and remembered how his wife had justified herself the evening before: "I'm so sorry, I just didn't see . . ." He shook his head in annoyance, as if his wife had invented dust herself, just to torment him. The coffee, which he swallowed with his usual gurgle, freed him from that thought. He turned on the radio. He liked to hear its voices in the background. He ate three or four cookies, dipping each one in his coffee with milk, and then began to clean. He went over the refrigerator's white surface again, then cleaned his study: the side of the bookshelf, above the door, between the knobs on the radiators. He cleaned the kitchen floor with a damp brush shaped like a broom, careful not to stir up any dust. He took a hot shower. But finally the bedroom was his cross to bear. He had not gotten to clean it since his wife had unleashed that awful chaos in her sleep. He took a piece of paper and left her a note on the table.

Dear Elena,

I didn't have time to clean the bedroom this morning, and it needs a good cleaning. I shouldn't say this, since what you do in your sleep isn't your fault, but just admit it: you were out of control this morning. I don't know what you were dreaming or how much you drank the night before, but I don't think having an episode like that is normal. It sends so many germs into the air. And the least you can do is take care of cleaning it today. After all, you made this mess by kicking up the air. But you ought to know how to clean it up yourself without making it worse. First you take off the comforter, then you beat it out on the balcony and lay it on the railing so it can air out. In the meantime you clean the surfaces: the nightstand, the dresser, and everything else, and obviously not with a dry cloth, or you'll just push the dirt around to a different spot. Spray the cloth with a few drops of cleanser, which is perfect for these things, or just do it with a damp cloth. Then mop the floor two or three times (including under the bed), and make sure the mop is wet enough but not dripping. Put the comforter back on and leave the window open for a half-hour. When you rinse out the mop, add a pinch of detergent and two sprays of ethyl alcohol to disinfect it.

Kisses,

Anselmo

He had a habit of leaving very precise instructions before he left the house. It calmed him down knowing that the note would make his wife feel obliged to take care of everything just as he said.

While Anselmo waited for the bus that morning, he thought about all the time that cleaning took up and felt like time was pressing in on him from all sides. But he had no choice. At every moment it was vitally important to do all he could to reduce the chaos in his home. At times the simple fact of leaving and then coming home at night comforted him, since he knew that, if he remained at home, he'd lose his mind in the most abject chores without ever accomplishing anything.

He arrived at work, greeted the lazy ladies with a slight nod, stamped his time card and shut himself away in his office for the entire morning. During his lunch break he returned to reading the Baldacchini, though his initial enthusiasm for it had worn off. He skipped the second chapter and went directly to the third, which sounded the most interesting. He lingered a long time over a page reproduced from the Gutenberg Bible, other pages from the original illuminated manuscripts, and the reproduced frontispieces. Then he realized there was a crucial problem with studying old books.

"How can I understand an old book without first knowing the milieu, the culture, the period that produced it?" he wondered, still looking at the reproduced pages in the book. "I can't. First I need context. Context." He repeated the word in his mind ten times. Now the question was how to face this problem of context. Before he took up the subject of the visual elements of old books he thought it would be good to have a deep understanding of humanism. As he thought about it, the book now closed in front of him, the face of Aldus Manutius appeared in his mind. "Aldus Manutius!" he said, striking his forehead with his palm. "There must be no better way to understand humanism than studying Aldus Manutius!" he said, surprised by his own stroke of genius. The name opened something new inside him. For one euphoric moment it seemed like the entire Italian humanist tradition was represented in Manutius's corpus of written work. Knowing this great writer's life was essential to studying this great book. In fact, he felt that some remnant of that editorial legacy was tingling inside him, between his chromosomes. Anselmo picked up the phone, looked up numbers for a few bookstores and soon was asking left, right, and center for books on Aldus Manutius. But no bookseller could immediately satisfy his curiosity. They all told him he'd have to wait at least a week, if not more, to have the book he asked for. Anselmo didn't have time to wait. He began writing in his notebook. Over and over he wrote Aldus Manutius's name, in a poor imitation of his watermark. He needed to know what motivated Aldus Manutius to publish a work like *The Dream of Poliphilus* by the Dominican friar Francesco Colonna in 1499. He wanted to read Manutius's biography, and by doing so, understand humanism itself: Manutius's relationship with Venetian culture, his friendship with Erasmus of Rotterdam, his use of cursive. He looked in a few online catalogs and found that under the name Aldus Manutius you could lose yourself in an enormous sea of books. One title stood out to him: it was about Aldus Manutius's relationship to Greek culture. The Alexandrian Library in Rome had a copy. He called the interlibrary loan office and said a patron needed it urgently.

"We need a faxed request," the librarian said from the other end of the line. Anselmo filled out a form and sent it.

He kept thinking about his own relationship to dust. "How long will I have to flail about, drowning in the world of the microscopic?" he wondered. Then he wrote this formula down in his notebook:

internal disorder = the search for external order

Under it he wrote:

Nothing in the world is so great and laudable that it can never turn to dust. In the end, every man becomes dust. In fact, his very body is already a gray mass of dust. Nothing is free from eventually becoming a dusty layer of air, from being spread by the wind and disseminated throughout the atmosphere. I'm waging war against little shreds of everything in the world.

Anselmo was very impatient the evening the book arrived from the Alexandrian Library in Rome. He began reading and didn't even notice when it was time to go home. He'd lived through two days of waiting as if it were a sort of fast before a feast. In the meantime he stared at the frontispiece in the Greek book's catalog. Gazing at its nearly illegible reproduction thrilled him so much that he almost wanted to share his joy with the lazy ladies. He didn't do this, but he felt he couldn't restrain the urge to share it with someone. He went to his computer and wrote an email to an old friend he hadn't seen for a year. He was named Paolo, just like Aldus Manutius's son.

How's life, Paolo? It's been so long since I've seen you. Your sons must have grown so much that I wouldn't recognize them. I'm well.

Every so often I have paralyzing neck pains, but otherwise I get by fine. You know, just admit it: there aren't that many things in the world to be happy about, but there are enough if you know how to get by. I forgot to mention that right now I'm reading a biography of Aldus Manutius and I found out his son was named Paolo, like you. Best wishes, and say hello to your family for me.

Anselmo

He immediately received the email right back, along with a notice that the address was wrong.

"Never mind then!" Anselmo said, shrugging his shoulders.

When he returned home, he ate something quickly and then shut himself away in his study to read the book on Aldus Manutius and Greek culture. Elena was unhappy because Anselmo hadn't appreciated her dinner enough, but was pleased to know that she could drink alone in the kitchen in peace, without her husband tormenting her. She made a Mandarin punch and listened to the radio on low while she worked on a drawing of animals running through a wood, which she would show to her children one day. She hadn't given up hope about having children one day, even if Anselmo had. Anselmo thought these drawings were little more than a useless pastime, not only because they presented a problem he didn't want to confront. That night he went to sleep at three-thirty with this eating away at him: "Would Aldus Manutius and his kind have respected the *Myriobiblos*?" Certain questions are here just to complicate our lives—questions for which, in reality, there is no true, historical answer.

He awoke that morning with the noble intention of finishing the chapter that very day. On his lunch break he went to his usual bar for a sandwich. He felt that people at the tables were secretly watching him, some of them even nudging each other to look at him. He went back into the library and sat at his desk. He was completely absorbed in reading and note-taking.

He checked the footnotes, looked up names in the index. At a certain point reading about Aldus Manutius's relationship to Greek culture became boring. He tried to make progress in it, but the more he read, the more it bored him. He hung, pensive, over the open book. He tried to imagine a colony of Greeks arriving in Venice from the Byzantine East at the beginning of the sixth century, but even this thought couldn't stimulate him. He was on page ninety-four, and there were some fifty pages left in the chapter. He still found the argument fascinating, yet he was too restless to read any further. He stroked his eyebrows, separating the hairs. Then he started pulling them out, first one, then another, then more. He dropped them one by one on the open page of his book on Aldus Manutius's relationship to Greek culture. He saw a word on the page pierced by a brown hair curved like a half-moon, and he tried to imagine a colony of Greeks in Venice at the beginning of the sixth century. He kept pulling out hairs for about fifteen minutes, still trying to think of those Greeks from the Byzantine East. Then he collected all the hairs along the binding, between pages ninety-four and ninety-five. He'd amassed a conspicuous wad of brown hair, and gazed at it, satisfied. Finally he closed the book, trapping all the hairs inside. He closed the book in his hands and sat for a few moments, flipping it over and over. He liked to think that someday someone interested in Aldus Manutius's relationship to Greek culture would turn to that page and be confronted with his wad of brown hair. He got up from the table and stood looking thoughtfully out the window. He waited for his lunch break to end. When the younger of the lazy ladies arrived he stared into her face as she passed, as if he needed to read something written in the lines that appeared on her forehead whenever she furrowed her brow to make herself look thoughtful because someone was looking. This woman plucked her eyebrows constantly, and Anselmo noticed that nothing remained of them except a very faint line of tiny hairs, which she thickened every day with a black make-up pencil.

"Here," Anselmo told the lazy ladies, handing her the book on Aldus Manutius and Greek culture. "You need to get this ready to go back to the Alexandrian Library in Rome."

She looked at it absently. Without saying yes or no, she took the book clumsily, placed it in an envelope, and handed it back to him. Anselmo wrote the library's address on the envelope and handed it to her a second time. She kept staring back at Anselmo.

"I'll send it tomorrow," she finally said.

No one could've imagined that a minuscule, insignificant part of Anselmo's body would be sent back to the Alexandrian Library that day between pages ninety-four and ninety-five of that book. Anselmo shut himself in his office and wrote on a sheet of paper: *There are those who believe that librarians need not read books. In my case it's very simple: there are books that do not want to be read by me.*

He returned to cataloging, trying to focus as much as possible on the rules of cataloging themselves. He repeated out loud: "asterisk, title, point, space, line, space . . ." It seemed to him that his own life was a fiction so absurd he couldn't handle it. At one point, the older of the lazy ladies appeared at his side to ask him something about circulation. Anselmo told her to make do, that by now she should be able to make those decisions on her own, but still she had no intention of taking responsibility. She laid the book she was holding on a colleague's desk and left his office, half-closing the door. Anselmo felt an overwhelming need to explain it to her, since he couldn't just go along with whatever she decided. Why had Aldus Manutius's relationship to Greek culture become a goal for its own sake to him? He tried to put his situation into words, and came up with a justification that, at first blush, seemed convincing: no one had ever doubted whether he ought to be a librarian, even if he had a gaping deficiency when it came to old books. Even if he saw himself as little more than a simple warehouseman, they all basically considered him a terrific librarian.

"I'm a librarian who has never seen an old book because I work with modern books, and so what? Anyway, I'm a librarian and no one has ever questioned my position, even if I don't follow the professional literature as I should, and I don't finish reading the Baldacchini or the book on Aldus Manutius's relationship to Greek culture." He picked up the book that the older of the lazy ladies had left on his desk. He stood up with the book in his hand and slid it across the counter.

"Take care of this. I'm not here to do your job for you," he told her smugly.

"Sure," the lazy lady answered through her teeth. Anselmo felt a mixture of joy and disgust inside him.

After closing he returned home and shut himself in his study. Elena asked him whether he preferred meatballs or the usual saffron rice for dinner. Anselmo didn't answer. He felt robbed, as if some part of his insides had been ripped out. He went into the bathroom, picked up the bottle of detergent, and poured out a bit of that thick, bluish liquid into the sink. Then he took a sponge and began to clean. It seemed like a lifetime since he'd cleaned the sink. He did the same with the rest of the bathroom. Finally, before shutting himself back in his study, he scoured the hidden corners of the hallway, where air currents from all over the house ran together.

"I didn't hear whether you wanted meatballs or rice," his wife said.

"Do whatever you want. Just leave me alone!" He slammed the door.

He wanted to try sending his old friend Paolo another note, this time from his home computer.

Listen, Paolo—

I've never understood what I'm doing here, in this world, in this dust-covered mortality. I can stand the neck pains. I'm a poor introvert who works in a filthy country library patronized by readers hungry for adventure, by the old who read newspapers and children who thumb through the encyclopedias to do their homework. Tell me, if you're still my friend, what am I doing here? Why did I think I could be of use to society if I suddenly started studying old books? What is the point of knowing that Aldus Manutius got his emblem of an anchor and a dolphin from Pietro Bembo, or whoever else? And then, with all the grief and chaos in the world, who would ever want me to study old books?

The door of the study opened very softly. Elena appeared, with tears in her eyes. She blew her nose a few times. Anselmo watched her, speechless.

"What is it?"

"Nothing," Elena said, swallowing her tears.

"Nothing?"

"Yes."

"Are you drunk?"

"No, I'm not drunk."

"Well, what do you want from me?"

"I want to tell you something."

"What?"

"Well, I'll tell you some other time."

"Now let me be," Anselmo said with an air of finality, drumming his fingers on the keyboard and gesturing at the screen. "I'm writing."

She tried once, then a few more times, to begin a sentence. She left the study, closed the door and went to the kitchen, her face buried in a handkerchief. Anselmo kept writing the email that she'd interrupted.

Look around and it seems that you cannot go on living in this revolting world. But then you get up in the morning, do your cleaning, look down and see the floor is clear of every speck of dust, and life is possible again. So you take a hot shower. You look at the filth running down the shower drain and think how you brought all that filth there on your own skin. And who knows where it goes, when the water and snarls of soap carry it away?. You cheer up and feel at ease again. Then you get ready for work. From that moment on everything collapses relentlessly. It's as if everything you'd taken such great care to build suddenly turned weak and flimsy. You open the window and a fine cloud of dust floats lazily around you, its particles swirling within a single beam of sunlight. And you leave for work, thoroughly pissed off. Everything is infuriating. Being a librarian is infuriating, and not being one is just as infuriating. Having to clean the house is infuriating, and not having cleaned the house is infuriating. When someone asks you something, you answer, "Get off my back." In short, you must fight a meticulous battle for your own survival. You want to draw up an army to fight alongside you, but then your realize that it's not at all like you'd thought, that they aren't fighting for your survival at all. They're fighting against you, so you send them off to take a shit, you barricade yourself in and shield yourself from the beasts that want to maul you, and from everything else.

He signed the email in capital letters and sent it. Thirty seconds later it bounced back, with a notice that it had been sent to a nonexistent address.

Do you know what I mean? he wrote back. *You can go fuck yourself.*

This email bounced back again, with the notice as before: *The following addresses had permanent fatal errors . . . Host unknown . . .* So he added:

You and the rest of your family can go fuck yourselves.

Then he turned off his computer. He rinsed off his hands and face, and went into the kitchen.

"Why are you crying?" he asked his wife, who was still crying alone, resting her head on the table and blasting her nose into a tissue like a trumpet.

"Because of how alone I feel," she answered without meeting his eyes.

"You too? I knew it!"

Anselmo looked around him. There were no meatballs or saffron rice on the table, just a bottle of vodka and one of the magazines Elena had been flipping through the night before. He opened the sideboard, took out three slices of bread, which he spread with mustard and olive spread.

"You're eating bread?" Elena asked.

"Is that okay with you?"

"I didn't have time to cook yet."

"Don't worry about it."

They sat in silence for ten minutes.

"Anselmo, how did we get this bad?"

"I don't know."

"You know what? I could be happy if I only knew what you wanted from me."

"I've been thinking that surrounding myself with old books might have been the worst idea I've ever had. What do you think?"

"If you say so."

"They're so dusty! The paper ages, the leather ages. Everything ages, even the ideas. Why should I do this to myself, suffocate myself with all this dust?"

"You're right."

"Old books will drive you crazy."

"I agree, it's better to just drop things like that."

"But the other day you said just the opposite: that studying books without ever seeing an old one is like studying smoke and never knowing what fire is. Isn't that what you said?"

Elena picked up a slice of bread and spread it with mustard and olive spread.

"We could be happy if we made more of an effort," Anselmo said with his mouth full, sipping water to rinse out the taste of bread, mustard, and olive spread in his mouth.

"Sometimes it feels so hard!"

"But not impossible."

"Yes, you're right."

Elena had stopped crying and now stood before the window drying her face on the handkerchief.

Anselmo's alarm rang at six the next morning. He got up and went straight to the bathroom to rinse the sleep from his face. For some time he'd fantasized about two attractive librarians in miniskirts who handed out books to passersby and complimented him. Every so often he gave them a pat on the rear to remind them to be nice to the patrons. He went back to the foot of the bed where his wife was still asleep, breathing in and out heavily, as if she were at the bottom of a pit, struggling to inhale. He thought about how he'd react if she started kicking and flailing under the sheets again, trapping all the dried-out filth at the foot of the bed. He got down on the floor to look under the bed, in case he needed to go over it with a damp cloth, and he saw three cat-sized balls of dust that a single breath could blow one way or the other across the floor.

"Impossible," he said out loud, feeling himself turn into a bundle of nerves.

"What is it?" Elena asked sleepily, with her head still hidden under the sheets.

"You should see the filth we've been sleeping on top of every night. Then you'd stop thinking I'm a madman."

"I should? I've never thought about that," Elena said, suddenly more awake.

"Just look under here . . . Actually, it's better if you don't look. There are three dust balls rolling around like tumbleweeds. You know?"

"As soon as I get up I'll clean everything."

"That's what you said yesterday."

"I did clean yesterday. The wind blew all the dust back in," Elena said, chewing her nail.

Anselmo went into the kitchen and made coffee with milk. "The wind did it," he mocked her. "You think you can fool me like that?" He felt like throwing everything out the window: his marriage, his life, his apartment. Throwing everything out and starting over from the beginning. He went back to the bedroom. Elena was asleep again. He put one hand on his hip and tapped her arm with the other.

"I want you to know those dust wads under the bed could give you some awful lung diseases," Anselmo said, pointing at the floor. "They're always moving about and banding together, and growing by the hour. Pretty soon they'll rise up and send their germs into the air, and then the germs will creep into our noses and pores . . . they'll just force their way into you. There's nothing worse than those tiny, microscopic things when they band together and get big." He snickered.

"I see, Anselmo. I'll do it as soon as I get up. I swear, the floor is as clear as a mirror. Right now I'm sleeping."

"There are some things I don't want to have to say over and over again, and since you have more time to dedicate to the house than I do, I'd appreciate it if you could take a bit more care. Otherwise, we might end up trapped in one giant dust ball someday. Do you understand?"

"Yes, of course. I'll do it."

"How will you do it?"

"Like you just said." Elena buried her head under the comforter again.

"But I haven't told you how to do it."

"Haven't you?"

He went back to the kitchen for coffee. He picked up the half-full bottle of vodka and put it away. But on the table he could still see sticky spots, which he wiped up with a paper towel. Then he went into his study and locked the door, setting a cactus close to the computer to absorb the electromagnetic rays. He stood and stared at the cactus for a few minutes, struggling to regain his senses. He turned on the computer and started a new email.

Look, Paolo, I can't do this anymore. The all-powerful air is threatening me, slipping its poisonous tentacles in and out every window. These twisting spirals of crazed particles commandeer everything in this house with a flat enough surface, roaring silently the whole time. I feel as though a puff of air could blow me into ruin (the harbor where all we common mortals end up). Before long my temples will be streaked and stained with gray, and I still won't have my life in order.

He got up from his seat, opened the door, and went back into the bedroom. Elena still hadn't gotten up. He wanted to wake her up himself to give her a few more orders for cleaning the room. He went back into his study. The dark screen of his computer was dotted with a few stars that seemed on the point of popping out at him. He nudged the mouse, and his latest e-mail appeared. He filled in his friend Paolo's address and hit send. The message bounced back. He turned off his computer and went to take a hot shower.

That day at work he cataloged and cataloged, not even lifting his eyes from the screen. He finished book after book and added them to the dizzying, tottering stack. From each book he pulled out the index card listing precisely where it belonged, and inserted it into the card file. In theory, the older of the two lazy ladies should've been entering the index cards and ordering the books, but Anselmo did most of them himself because she never took any initiative, not even on matters that were her sole responsibility. He preferred doing it himself, so that he didn't have to remind her every time there were books waiting. Anselmo didn't mind having piles of books overpower his desk, since working through the stacks made him feel at ease, more distracted from his colleagues and more in harmony with that new order he introduced by codifying them accurately. He compared himself to a simple mortician sorting bodies for burial according to their profession. "Squeeze them in as close as you can, even if they hated each other! And if books can be ordered and cataloged, it feels like everything in life can be just as organized," he thought.

At four-twenty his wife called, saying a vacuum cleaner salesman had stopped by with an interesting offer.

"I already told you, I don't want to hear a word about vacuum cleaners," Anselmo said, annoyed.

"But this one's different, believe me. It's like a spaceship. I saw it. It's beautiful, and it has so many filters that the air comes out completely clean."

"Sure," Anselmo groaned.

"Well, have you looked under the bed? If you look there now you won't believe your eyes. This gadget just sucked up everything as if it were never there, in the blink of an eye."

"You used the vacuum to clean under the bed?"

"Yeah, to see if it could pick up everything."

"Then you didn't clean it right after you got up, you just cleaned it because someone put a vacuum in your hands."

"If you look under the bed now, it looks just like a mirror."

"And what if it just spits the air back out, and that filth lands all over the bed?"

"I told you, the air that comes out is so clean that you could put your face in it."

"Stop repeating that crap."

"Now you won't even believe what I say. It has a filtering system so good that not even a speck of dust can get through."

"And you believe that?"

"Really, the salesman told me, we can leave the curtains on the windows and even the Persian rug on the floor, because this vacuum can clean everything in two seconds."

"Don't even mention the curtains. We're not discussing those again, and you can forget about the rug," he answered, irritated. He recoiled from the phone in disgust, as if to distance himself from this revolting suggestion.

"Look, this is exactly what it says: capable of holding ninety-nine point ninety-seven percent of particles thicker than zero point zero-zero-zero three millimeters. And there's more: they guarantee effective protection against allergens and bacteria, and it returns the air cleaner than it was before," his wife reported. She enunciated *allergens* and *bacteria* slowly, cutting off each syllable.

"Whatever, tell him to come by when I'm home," Anselmo said, shifting in his seat.

"I already told him to come by when you're here."

"Anyway," Anselmo finally said, "it would nice if, instead, you could scrub under the bed with a damp cloth. You know, when you don't clean with water, it smells like death under the bed and it makes my hair stand up straight."

Elena started laughing, silently so her husband couldn't hear. She added, "It always smells like death in our bed. It's enough to make you feel dead just taking a nap."

After he hung up the phone, Anselmo closed the book he'd been cataloging and rested his hand on the cover. He thought of one evening when he and his mother had sat on a bench under the awning outside Porto Catinari Station in a pouring rain. He propped his head on his hands, his elbows perched on top of a violin case on his lap. He felt as if he'd be there forever. He watched little streams of water running down the street. Sitting across from Anselmo was another boy about the same age, wearing a blue sailor suit with dripping wet shoulders. He was also with his mother, but seemed indifferent to everything she said, as he pouted and let his shoes fill up with water. At a certain point his mother got up from the bench to ask Anselmo's mother if her son was a *violinist* in an orchestra. Anselmo's mother answered yes, that her son was a *violinist*, and set one hand on Anselmo's disheveled hair.

"I knew right away that that case meant a *violinist*."

"And your son?" Anselmo's mother asked her.

"My son is a *pianist*," the other mother said. "But this evening he wasn't in great form. He woke up a bit nervous today. I'm afraid something might be off."

"It's natural that he'd be nervous."

While the two mothers discussed their sons' health and states of mind, the *violinist* and the *pianist* started to look each other up and down, without saying a word or taking their eyes off each other. When the train arrived the mothers and sons found an empty compartment. The *pianist* stood up on the seat, his shoes so soaked that his every footfall came down like a conqueror's. He was chewing bubblegum, and every so often would blow an enormous bubble and hold it until his mother told him to stop. In the compartment, the two *musicians* kept studying each other, not saying anything. Then, the *pianist* started to blow his largest bubble yet, swallowing the air inside it, without his mother noticing. Then Anselmo got up, leaving his violin case on the seat, and slapped *the pianist* on the cheek. The *pianist*'s bubble popped, leaving his face covered in sticky gum. The *pianist*'s mother said nothing, but, from the way she cleaned her son's face, seemed truly irritated at what the *violinist* had done. Then the boys kept staring at each other without saying a word until they burst into laughter like madmen. They burst out of the compartment and ran down the aisle of the train car, their mothers' shouts chasing them.

"What's your name?" asked the *pianist*, who was leading the way.

"Anselmo. And yours?"

"Giovanni, but everyone calls me Ciccio."

Just like Anselmo's home computer, his work computer's screen was dotted with stars with tiny, glowing points that made Anselmo's eyes hurt. He checked his watch and got up to walk around the reading room. He walked slowly along a line of books ordered by subject, scratching his chin and sinking deeper and deeper in thought. While he studied their different-colored spines he kept remembering that train ride along the Adriatic Coast. If he'd once been that child, that *violinist*, then the abyss between his childhood and his current life was so great that he almost felt like a man without a past. He glanced at his watch. He went back into his office thinking that he'd never know his childhood self again.

Five minutes before quitting time he rinsed his face in the library bathroom and rubbed rose lotion on his hands. With a comb he kept in the library bathroom he combed his hair back. Then he took a piece of paper and rubbed the toes of his shoes so they'd look polished again. He took his brown overcoat off the coatrack and put it on, pulling it snug around his neck. Then he put on his hat and looked at his watch. There was still one minute until he could stamp his time card. He waited, watching his colleagues chatting among themselves, losing patience as he walked back and forth wringing his hands.

At one minute past seven that evening Anselmo was on his way home. As he walked he looked up at the buildings' corroded facades, at the crane that filled the thin sliver of sky between them, as he had many times before. He said hello to the newsstand cashier, waited ten or fifteen minutes for the bus, punched his ticket, and sat in the middle of the car. The bus rocked back and forth, and the street outside seemed unchangeable, the same as always. There were cigarette butts on the ground and people groggy after a day of work. From time to time he felt trapped in his own little town, relegated to his daily routine, with nothing possible but the usual.

He stopped under a flickering stoplight, then crossed the street that brought him to his own street. For the first time he noticed that on the edge of the sidewalk stood a dusty tree that had grown up, strained, through a crack. It looked disheveled, but it had survived, and all of existence seemed to cling to its lonely arms. "There are so many men who feel the same way," Anselmo thought. "They're like plants that force their way up through the cracks in the cement. They have no water and no one to care for them, but still they grow tall and strong."

He opened the front door and put on his slippers.

"Finally!" cried Elena, waving a vacuum cleaner manual as she greeted her husband.

Anselmo listened with rapt attention as his wife told him enthusiastically of this strange new machine. She showed him photos and instructions, everything the salesman had given her.

"It could all be true. But I've never had any faith in vacuums like that."

"But it could solve all our problems. At least think about it."

"Yeah, if everything works how the salesman tells you it will! Don't hold your breath."

After dinner he shut himself away in his study to read the vacuum cleaner manual. Then he wrote to his old friend.

Dear Paolo,

Dust is insidious. It piles up, it grows, it always comes back worse. We're all constantly wasting away, constantly losing hair, flakes of skin, and everything else. Our own windows and doors let in the most inconceivable things, whether carried by the wind or on our shoes and clothes. Our rugs, carpets, pillows, and mattresses are patches of garbage that spawn their own strange creatures. Some of us are allergic to these creatures that crap at strategic points all over the house to torment our lungs.

But what about the meteor showers that rain through our atmosphere, spreading germs from outer space? The atmosphere, as you know better than I, is an ocean in perpetual motion: it ebbs and flows with waves rising and falling, mixing every little thing up with it. We look up at the sky as if the heavens were clear and transcendent. But that air that covers this earth is filled with tiny creatures of every kind, so much that dust in the wind is the only thing truly multicolored and multiethnic, multicentered and multicenturied, multiformed and multijointed. It's also the thing most difficult to classify, on the earth and throughout space. It is what, finally, is most cosmopolitan and cosmoplanetary . . .

Everything superficial actually has so much depth to it, that sometimes it seems like everything must in fact be its opposite.

He leaned back and looked at his entire text at once. He pressed enter and waited a few seconds. This time two emails returned immediately with an annoying *ping*: the one he wrote before he left home that morning, and the one he'd just written. Both had a message saying his old friend Paolo's email address didn't exist. Anselmo shrugged and started laughing.

When he came out of his study, he found his wife sitting in the kitchen, listless, her hair hanging in her eyes. She'd become tired of everything. She hardly left the house anymore, and when she did it was just to get things from the supermarket, or from the Saturday market, which she always looked forward to. She walked to the town square calmly, in no hurry. She liked hearing the vendors shout out what they had, even though she didn't buy much. When it rained, and the market was canceled, she'd walk along the street that led there to look in the shop windows. Anselmo would only stand at the street's center divider for a bit, since he thought things like this weren't necessary. The wool sweaters usually set him off.

"I've told you a thousand times that I hate that wool. Why do you still insist on buying these rags? It's driving me crazy." He knew he was becoming more and more stubborn and insufferable. "Just don't complain to me when the house is full of lint."

The angrier Elena was, the more neutral her tone. She stayed silent, looking out the window. She poured herself a drink of vodka and said, "You're right, Anselmo. It was on sale, so I thought . . . but I'll be careful about the lint. I'll keep it under control. You'll see."

Later that night Anselmo walked over to his wife, stroked her hair, and picked up the bottle of vodka.

"I can't watch you ruin yourself like this."

Elena turned and looked her husband up and down. She wanted to believe she was strong enough to handle what she wanted to tell him. A feeling of oppression rose up inside her. Dense and warm, it filled her stomach, chest, and arms. It spread over her skin and she couldn't speak. She had a cross-eyed look and heavy eyelids. Anselmo noticed her face was flushed and her forehead was dripping with sweat.

"You know," he said, seeing Elena grip her knees with both hands, "I read that manual. I found it pretty interesting."

She raised her head slightly to shift the hair out of her eyes. She didn't understand a word he was saying.

"I'm talking about that instruction manual for the new vacuum cleaner," Anselmo went on.

"Ah!"

"I think you're right, it seems like it might be a great thing. At least someone understands the problem we have. And then, building something to get rid of household dust is already an important step forward, don't you think? A tool like this but with vapor would be more useful, because, as you know better than me, a particle of dust is nothing but a particle of air with most of the water dried out of it. The moment you cover it with vapor, the dust weighs down heavier and passes from its dry state to a humid one, and in doing so it avoids the various flits and flutters that can cause us so much worry. Do you understand, Elena? Anyway, I think this kind of vacuum cleaner would help us by itself, even if it works dry and can't avoid sending a few specks up in the air and letting them end up on the pillows and the furniture."

Elena got another glass of vodka. This time she pushed her hair out of her face, revealing two red, shiny eyes that gazed, bewildered, into space. She tried to put an end to the situation and make her head stop spinning.

"I'm your friend, Anselmo, and I believe everything you tell me."

"But that's an evasive statement."

"No, love, you're wrong. I love you so much," she said, holding back tears.

Anselmo looked at the ground, then reached out and this time it was he who pushed the black hair out of her eyes.

"I love you too," he said, but he was disoriented. He no longer knew what foundation there was to support those words.

Elena remained seated, watching her husband as if his words had opened a window into the past. Then she remembered how Anselmo used to walk to her house with his violin and leave it on a chair, and she'd take advantage of it to slip a love note inside the case for him to read at home or on the bus. Elena got up from her chair, took Anselmo's hand, and squeezed it. She brushed against his lips as if she wanted to reclaim the image of her husband that time had taken upon itself to push further and further into the past.

"You know, Anselmo, I'd rather be wrong with you than right with someone else," she said, lowering her eyelids.

Anselmo dropped his hands and remained speechless, scratching his head while his wife finished the rest of her vodka. Then she invited her husband, taking him by the hand, out onto the balcony. She shut the window and they stood in silence, looking into the dark. It was a silence in which every single noise took on visible lines. The wind blew in from the hills, driving the scent of onions toward the sea. Anselmo took two steps away from his wife, set his hands on the railing, and looked up at the smallest stars in the sky.

"Do you ever feel like there are tiny hidden creatures that cut through the atmosphere and blow about in the wind while they fall toward the earth?"

"No."

"And do you ever feel that even in this very breeze, the scent of onions is only there to hide what is really gunpowder?"

"No."

"Then what do you feel?"

"Just loneliness."

"I feel loneliness too."

They stayed there silently, Anselmo with his hands on the railing and Elena holding herself tight.

"Do you feel alone because you drink or do you drink because you feel alone?"

"No, I feel alone because I feel alone."

"Maybe it would be good for us if we could go to Ponza for a day," Anselmo said, after a pause.

"To do what?"

"They say Ponza has nice beaches."

"I didn't know that."

"Really, and there are some beaches you can only reach by boat. You think they're beautiful?"

Elena opened the balcony door and went back into the kitchen. She moved slowly, scratching her head. She sat down at the table and started sketching her little animals.

Anselmo shut himself away in his study, turned on his computer and wrote another email.

Dear Paolo,

I told you in my last email that fine atmospheric dust is what makes it so we can see the blue sky, and even the light diffused through the air. In fact, the sunlight that reaches our atmosphere has been intercepted, diffused, and disseminated by countless grains of weightless dust that are dragged along by the wind. These grains are so minute that sometimes they look smaller than the waves of light themselves. And I wonder, how can our atmosphere let in that crust of the universe floating through outer space? If friction is a major factor in dust, could it be that the sky, with its celestial turns, is wearing itself thinner every day and its scraps are falling on us as dust? We can't delude ourselves, you see. There's no escape on earth. Wherever we go we'll always find dust piles that swarm in the strangest orbits—tiny creatures that spin endlessly, that mix and reshuffle in a thousand different patterns, that bounce off each other, that push each other away. So we accept it and live with this disquieting presence that swims over our heads and floods under our feet.

What else, if not dust, can show us that ever-present boundary between the visible and invisible, between existence and nothingness? Anyway, and in conclusion, the more I clean up dust, the further away death seems.

Part II

Over the next few days the stack of books that Anselmo didn't have time to catalog grew taller and taller on his desk. Some of these were recent acquisitions, like some twenty volumes he'd had purchased from an old library on the brink of shutting down. He'd let some books sit there out of sheer laziness, mostly minutes from ecclesiastical conventions, local poetry collections, or cookbooks that local housewives were always donating. Sometimes he'd open a book at random and run his eyes over the words, without even comprehending their meaning. Then he'd put it back and pick up another, then another. He knew the flaps of every last one. But the thought of cataloging for years and years made the shoes of a librarian feel too tight. On some days he truly resented cataloging, loathed it for how mechanical it was. It kept him from crossing over the threshold of the frontispiece and entering the life of the text. Besides, reading librarians' trade magazines flooded him with doubt. Everything about his profession was changing, the magazines said, even its very name. He could no longer call himself a mere librarian. All of his peers were reinventing themselves as *managers of knowledge* with specific domains of expertise, and he needed to do the same. But Anselmo couldn't see himself as a manager, not at all. The thought that he had to become a *manager* to lend his work more credibility only made him shake his head.

The days passed, and from time to time Anselmo felt the urge to write his old friend Paolo about his life, what he did, what he thought. He even wrote about his coworkers:

On the eve of the apocalypse those two degenerates will still be talking about their pensions and bank accounts.

But for this friend he didn't feel the need to sketch out any lives but his own.

We have reason to hold that life may be something more than this cluster of particles aging day by day, something more than this conglomerate of facts, emotions, cares . . . Something more than what we see, but still something less . . .

When the message returned to sender he sat silent a moment, his elbows propped on the desk and his chin in the palm of his hand. He fixated on the wall and barely raised his gaze from the screen: *you're not there, but one day you will be*, he wrote in his mind. Then he shot out of his chair, grumbling and gazing out the window at the building next door. Sometimes he picked up a book and flipped it over, then flipped it back and sat down again. Other times he'd cut out newspaper articles and tape them behind the door, then remove them and throw them out when he grew tired of seeing them. One day he indulged one of his most bizarre ideas: he wrote up a proposal for a new collection on entomology, and submitted it to Catinari's city cultural commissioner, a man who'd always made Anselmo feel a bit reticent and shy.

"I'll read this as soon as I can," the cultural commissioner said, sitting in an armchair fit for Louis XIV, as if he were delivering an edict for all of history. Anselmo looked at the man's slump, and the way he seemed to blend into the back of his armchair, and thought of an arctic animal settling in for a long hibernation.

A week later the cultural commissioner called him in to give his definitive answer. Again slumped in his armchair with a very severe cold, he spoke in a nasal voice, constantly sneezing. Anselmo leaned back and listened: "I'd prefer that my staff take their jobs more seriously and think like real librarians. Who could possibly be interested? You think Catinarians would sit down and read this stuff? Do me a favor, for once!"

As the commissioner continued to expound on his reasons for

refusing to create an entomological collection, Anselmo noticed a light flouring of dandruff on the shoulders of the man's jacket. He stood up and gestured to his own shoulders, to indicate the man had something disgusting there. The commissioner looked first at one shoulder, then the other. Finally he took off his jacket and said, "Oh, it must be pollen from the mimosas."

But Anselmo wasn't stupid and it wasn't hard to see that that flour could only be dandruff. From that day forward, Anselmo didn't speak to the commissioner again. He felt crestfallen. The lazy ladies, who took note of every little shift in Anselmo's habits and emotional state, began to suspect that something in his life had changed. He worked less efficiently and the order that had once ruled his office was now slightly askew. More than once they noticed crumpled pieces of paper in the trash can, empty caramel boxes on the floor under the coatrack, or banana peels rotting on the desk. Sometimes he even forgot to turn off the computer or close the windows. One morning they saw him refuse to let a class of schoolchildren visit the library.

"Why would children ever need to visit a library? What would they do here? This isn't a theme park!" he told the teacher.

He was despondent and impatient, and yet completely unaware of it himself. He had no idea he was changing. He went on leading his small-town life of quiet desperation, finding a dull serenity in comfortable habits.

When time accelerates, we must live more slowly and shelter ourselves from any kind of frenzy. You may not believe me, dear Paolo, but I maintain that a town like this, that makes you yearn to flee its flat provincialism, may be the only place you can still know humanity. I, for one, can't reconcile these two opposing wills.

One Monday morning they saw him come into the office, more stooped than usual, with an untrimmed beard and bags under his eyes. His face was more discolored and his hair more unkempt than they'd ever seen. The two women shared a glance and snickered. They found something strange in Anselmo's gestures, something bizarre, even comical in his comportment and way of looking at things. That morning he stamped his time card and shut himself away in his office.

I write: Nihil sub sole novi, *and I ask myself: do you believe that saying? Have you ever opened a window at nine in the morning and seen how the sunlight slants through the glass? Have you seen the thousands of crazed particles flying back and forth in that beam of light? Has this never made you think of sperm, or of the way all matter is constantly breaking down? What are all those particles? What is the sunbeam that falls through a window even made of?*

He kept thinking, rubbing his cheeks. The sound of shaving annoyed him. He wasn't used to feeling his beard after two or three days without shaving. He got up, took some long, wide steps, then leaned his elbows on the windowsill. He sat back down at his desk. A little later, the elder of the lazy ladies came in to bring him the city council newsletter and found Anselmo absorbed in a small book from which he didn't raise his gaze. Anselmo's indifference made the woman comfortable. She lowered her voice, so low she was almost apologizing.

"I'll leave this here," she said, setting the newsletter on the desk.

Anselmo snatched the newsletter brusquely, opened it at random, and tossed it back on the desk.

"Throw it out," he spat back without looking at her, barely raising his eyes to see if she moved. Her nervous tic, which typically was almost imperceptible, grew worse. Now her eye was twitching as if she wanted to beat away an insect buzzing around it.

The woman stood still.

"But—it's the city council newsletter. How can I just throw it away?" she said, with that annoying *s* between her teeth.

"Like this," Anselmo replied. He got up from his chair, picked up the newsletter, and threw it in the trash himself. "See?" He pulled it out of the trash and threw it back in. "Easy!"

"This isn't funny," she said.

"Then go, and close the door on your way out. Can't you see I'm reading?"

The woman left the office, closed the door, and went to lean against the radiator with her other coworker. She told her everything that had just happened, heightening the drama and lingering on every slightest detail. They agreed that Anselmo was going through a difficult time, and may even be suffering a nervous breakdown. One of them was inclined to think his wife's character had caused it, since who knew when or for what strange reason she ever came out of the house. The other lady thought that deep down Anselmo wanted a management role and, now that he'd definitively broken with the cultural commissioner, believed he'd lost all hope of being promoted.

As the two women wondered what had caused Anselmo's emotional state, a stranger walked in. He was thin, and bundled up snugly in a velvet coat with a scarf up to his eyes and a hat on his head. He had oval-shaped glasses and a surgeon's little leather suitcase. He didn't take off his hat, but bowed his head forward and asked politely, with an air that was studied but not too much so, if he could take a look at the shelves. He spoke with a foreign accent that seemed French or Spanish.

"Go ahead," said one of the lazy ladies. The other one, however, not at all used to this type of gallantry, merely waved toward the long wall of books in the front.

"Thanks," said the stranger, emphasizing the *s* a bit too much.

The man left his little leather suitcase on a chair and turned toward the shelves. He walked slowly, with his left shoulder slightly tilted, as if he'd suffered some malady or accident which had never fully healed. He handled the books like someone with an instinct for organizing. He picked up each one, read the cover page, checked the call number, and put it back in place, taking care to line it up with the others. When he finished walking the length of that shelf, he went to the general catalog and searched for titles he'd written in a small notebook. He came back to the counter and turned to one of the women, who already expected he'd make some request she wouldn't know how to complete. He seemed like the meticulous type who didn't miss anything. He politely asked the woman for a book that was listed in the general catalog but not found on the shelves, and showed her the call number. She went to the shelf and returned with a book, but he pointed out that it wasn't the book he asked for, and that the call number corresponded to another title in the catalog. The woman checked the catalog herself and found the man was right.

"And it has to be that one?"

"Yes."

"Then let's try to resolve this. Please wait here a moment. I'll go get the manager."

"Go ahead, I'll wait."

The woman knocked on the door of Anselmo's office. When he didn't respond, she opened it just far enough to tell him she couldn't find a book that a patron had requested. Anselmo slightly sarcastically scolded his coworker who would never assume responsibility for anything. He carelessly tossed the little book he was reading off to one corner of the desk and shot up from his chair. He went into the main hall, greeted the man, and listened to his problem.

"I'm looking for this title, *Green Mansions*, translated by Montale," the man said, pointing his notepad, where he'd written the author's name. "But she says this call number corresponds to *The Purple Land*."

"Then there must be some error. Let's go look under the author," Anselmo said, again addressing his coworker, but knowing that she'd go lean on the radiator and the task would now be all his. "Let's see if we can find it by searching for the author."

He went to the shelf and found the right book immediately.

"It's this, right?"

"Exactly," the man said, taking the book in his hand and thanking the librarian for his thoughtfulness.

"You're welcome to read here, if you want," Anselmo said, gesturing to the empty tables in the middle of the room. "You can see there is room."

The stranger looked at the tables and then back at Anselmo.

"Excuse me, but I'd prefer to take it home," he said finally, without showing the slightest sign of worry. "Here there is too much pelusa for my taste."

"Excuse me?" asked Anselmo, who didn't understand the word pelusa.

"Just look!" The man walked over to a table and ran his finger along it to show the dust.

Anselmo stood aghast. No one had ever pointed dust out to him before. It was like a punch in his stomach. He bent down to see it in the light and saw the trail this man's finger left on the table.

"You're right. I hadn't realized how dirty it was. Sometimes our cleaning staff isn't very thorough . . . What can I say? They're thinking about something else, instead of what they're paid for," Anselmo said, feeling for himself the light dust that clothed the table like a lining. He wanted to make the man understand that it wasn't the first time he'd noticed the cleaning staff's deficiency. But the man waved his hand to show he had no interest in these concerns. He only said, "I understand." Then he took a book from the shelf at random, the first one his hand touched, and flipped through it rapidly. The pages emitted a cloud of dust that dissolved in front of his face.

"Do you see?" the man said, gesturing at the jumble of particles that was now flitting about all around them and dissolving little by little in the air. "Let's share our space with an infinite number of invisible particles. Man is inclined toward great things, but it's the small things, this silent matter, which always slips out of our hands."

"I see," said Anselmo, who was trying to cut through that cloud of molecules with his hand, as if it were a giant spiderweb.

"Then you agree with me?"

"Yes, of course. I already told you, our staff isn't very good."

Anselmo was terrified: if the stranger pointed out dust to him again, it would send him into a rage.

"Do you see why I prefer reading at home?"

"I can only admit you're right. So dust bothers you too?"

"Unfortunately, yes."

The man put the book back on the shelf, as if he were used to resigning himself to the presence of dust.

"You know, I can't stand it either, and I don't understand how the staff can just pass over it as if it were nothing."

"Because they don't see it. People aren't used to noticing small things, they pass right over them as if they were nothing. But for someone who notices, like you, the borders of things dilate a bit beyond the things themselves, and so you see the pelusa."

"The pelusa?"

"Of course, the pelusa. Look closely at the table."

"I see it, I see it. I still don't understand, though, with all the dust that we breathe and this pelusa that flits about and surrounds us, why infectious diseases aren't more common."

"Obviously we must be better protected than we think."

"But just look at it."

"That's the problem."

Anselmo looked the man up and down for the first time. The stranger looked about Anselmo's own age: the gaunt, slender face, the clear skin, the temples streaked with gray, the shirt buttoned up to his chin, and the green eyes that were calm but a bit sad. His movements were a little clumsy, as if his very presence in the world were an accident. It was the first time he found someone else for whom dust was a central problem. And he was certain this man would understand if he told him he could never find peace as long as he was surrounded by dust.

"Out of curiosity," said Anselmo after he had finished watching him, "are you Argentine by any chance? I heard your accent . . ."

"Yes, I'm Argentine."

"From Buenos Aires?"

"Yes, from Buenos Aires."

"Wonderful! And how long have you been in Italy?

"Years."

The man jerked abruptly toward the window, as if he thought someone were calling him. Then he raised his eyes. Anselmo was watching him, rapt.

"And what brings you to Italy?"

"Excuse me, but may I borrow it?" the stranger interrupted, pointing to the book Anselmo had just found.

"No problem. You just have to fill out this card."

Despite the dust, the man leaned against the table as he filled out the card.

"We'll have to register you as a new user," Anselmo said. The man's tiny handwriting leaned slightly to the right.

The stranger squeezed the book into his coat pocket. As he headed for the door, one of the lazy ladies asked him to sign in. The stranger looked at the guestbook's three columns and took a pen from his inside pocket. In the first column he signed his name with an indecipherable scribble in the first column and wrote the date in the second. When he reached the third, "Profession," he hesitated.

"But I have no profession."

"Then write 'none,'" said the woman.

The man did as she said and left the pen on the book. The woman turned the book toward her, looked at the scrawl, and said in a reproachful tone, "Excuse me, sir. I'm very sorry, but could you sign in a legible manner, since no one can understand this?"

"My name is Adrián Bravi. Write it yourself if you care that much," he added, pointing to the first column.

"What did you say—Arián?"

"No, no, Adrián. Like Adriano but without the 'o' at the end. Adrián Bravi."

As the man spoke, the woman noticed he was missing one of his premolars. She wrote his full name in block letters and closed the book with the pen inside.

"Excuse me, could you give me back the pen, please? It was a gift and I'd be very sorry to lose it."

The woman took the pen and returned it to him without looking him in the eye.

"Just remember you have a month to return the book."

The man lifted his hat slightly in a kind of salute, giving them a glimpse of his incipient baldness, and then walked away slowly. Anselmo took the card he'd just filled out and shut himself in his office. He stretched his legs out under his desk again and read in a low voice, "Adrián Bravi, Argentine, 31 via dei Marini . . ."

He looked at the clock. It was almost noon. He untied his shoes, loosened his collar, felt a drop of sweat form under his arm and trickle down along his ribs. He opened the window that looked out on the street. *Pelusa, pelusa, pelusa,* he wrote mentally while he walked up and down through the office. Never had a word fit so perfectly. He found it so consonant with what he himself intended to express that he inserted it into his vocabulary without knowing what it really meant. In any case, he wanted to check how it was translated in the library's Spanish-Italian dictionary: *peach fuzz, fluffy fabric* . . . He thought for a moment. He also consulted a Spanish-only dictionary. He looked for the entry pelusa and translated it, copying it down on a sheet of paper.

Very subtle and barely perceptible veil of fuzz, like that of a peach, that covers a person's face or even becomes a fabric itself. Agglomeration or gathering of the subtlest fibers of dust and hairs that, for example, forms under the furniture when one does not clean thoroughly.

This told him that, unlike dust, pelusa was a snarl of oily substances and mixed materials, an insidious mix entrusted to the air on its way throughout the world. He leaned in close to his computer and wrote:

Our destiny, Paolo, has always been clear: everything turns to dust. It's despairing to think that, before taking this form, my every individual particle, my every atom, flew throughout space with all the others, and formed stars, then comets, then planets and asteroids and who knows what else, and now it's here inside, tangled up between veins and nerves, and within a few years it will return as something else. We're a mass of particles dancing in the light. Everything hurtles through the wind like pelusa. This is the great condemnation of being human, of being someone on the earth that grows and wastes away.

When the message returned, Anselmo wrote another.

Paolo,

I've always thought life can't get better until the entire universe changes. Thousands of years later we're still sweeping up filth from the Big Bang. But now the time has come, we need an anti-Big Bang to suck back in all the nastiness that the crash flung all over the world. A Great Squeeze, then. Life would be marvelous. You could ask, 'what has dust got to do with it?' instead of 'what has it got to do with dust?' Just imagine. Dust rules the entire universe. I always say, I have two options to survive in this revolting world: close my eyes and resign myself to it, or plan an underground system of breathing tubes that suck the dust and garbage out onto the balcony. I'd be very happy if I saw nothing on the ground, nothing on my furniture, absolutely nothing at all. The problem is I'd need to clean the floor and make suction ports for the vacuums, which is a challenge I can't take on at the moment. It's hard not to see pelusa everywhere: everything is ruined, everything you wear is shattered into particles. How can you fail to notice when we live in chaos? And now that spring, that shadowy pollen season, is coming . . . And pollen, of course, comes from the Latin word for dust.

Indulge my curiosity: when you make love, do you think about dust? I ask because I can't get it out of my head, not even when I'm screwing. I just can't stand how the sheets go this way and that way on the bed and shove that morass of stagnant, inhuman decay out onto the ground.

He heard a knock on the door. He didn't answer right away. Adrián Bravi's voice echoed in his head: his Argentine accent, his way of speaking, his gestures. *Toc, toc, toc,* he heard once more.

"Go away," Anselmo said, barely moving from his keyboard.

It was one of the lazy ladies carrying a little leather suitcase, letting it swing slightly from side to side.

"It was the man who came before. He forgot this on his chair."

"Oh!" said Anselmo, annoyed by her presence. "But who knows? There could be a bomb inside."

She set the suitcase on the ground and immediately jerked herself back up. "Of course," she said. "We'd never expect something like that in a library, but then crime is rising."

Anselmo took the little leather suitcase, set it down gently on the desk and unzipped it. Inside there was a folder full of papers, a book, an agenda, and two ballpoint pens.

"It's nothing," he said, throwing it down with a mock sigh of relief.

"Holy Jesus, thank you," she said.

"Yes, thank me. You could already be plucking angels' wings in the afterlife by now."

"You scared me! That guy did seem a bit strange."

"Dying in this office with you would've been a very dismal end."

"Whatever," she said. "I'm going back to work."

Anselmo was about to put the things back in the little suitcase when he was abruptly seized by a curiosity to read the sheets sticking out the sides of the little notebook. He took the first sheet and read aloud, in a low voice:

Esteemed Professor Francesca Chiusaroli,

Thank you for honoring me with the gift of your book on the philosophical language of John Wilkins. I took the liberty of writing a brief review of it, which I sent yesterday to Taxonomi, *a magazine in Buenos Aires that I work with from time to time. I started by quoting the passage, 'The real is offered to men's eyes like a disordered, indistinct conglomerate, amounting to a recomposition of order beginning from chaos. To know it can only be done by enumerating, classifying, analyzing, and most importantly, naming entities. Then we might finally arrive at a universal grammar that might make possible the world inventory postulated by Wilkins. Your work, I believe, has identified the presupposition behind this task: restoring the real to order and reducing chaos through a language that could impose itself like a universal code of knowledge. It comes from asking: why this need to classify, to catalog, this activity of language on language?*

I enjoyed writing about your book. As soon as the review is published I will send you a copy.

A few lines below, the letter resumed with this postscript:

PS: I can't wait to see you again. I'm still struck by the zebra-striped bracelet you wore the last time we saw each other. I hope you wear it again.

My sweetest regards,

Adrián Bravi

Anselmo picked up some other pages held together with a paper clip and read, in the same tiny handwriting that leaned slightly to the right:

Brief essay on domestic taxonomy

Various instructions

Draw a grid in which you will segment all of the real, subjecting each individual thing to minute classification. Use language as your nomenclature and ask yourself, for example, what are the elements that make up the pelusa on your bathroom floor. List them, meticulously identifying each one. Compare that list with one for the pelusa on your bedroom floor, and determine which elements they have in common, and which differ. Then repeat these steps for the balcony, and compare that composite with the ones from the bathroom and bedroom, to confirm with certainty which elements come from outside and which come from within the home. This information is very important in deciding how to properly clean the home.

Start from the premise that nothing is covered by a surface. The outer shell is the thing itself. Then go on like this, from surface to surface.

You must not neglect another important fact: your every action, even within your own home, happens on a predetermined schedule . . . circadian rhythms dictate our activities, our models of behavior . . . we need to learn their schedules, and which activities produce more pelusa. Create a unit of measurement to quantify and monitor pelusa levels down to the nanogram.

What do you do at 4:30? Let's suppose you're at work in an armchair. At 5:30, get up, get out of the chair, and wipe down the floor with a white cloth. Measure the amount of pelusa on the cloth. At 12:30 do the same experiment in the kitchen and around the table, then try to determine the common elements as best you can . . . You'll find the components and amounts will differ every time. Classify the elements one by one, as a game, according to their principal category. If there is more of it in the bathroom, then when you take off your clothes before a shower, shake out the lint and hairs that were trapped between your pants and undershirt. Or you may find more of it around the table after dinner, or after you get out of bed . . . then replace all your wool and cotton upholstery with synthetic materials. Always check the percentage of polyamide . . . fragments of mineral, vegetable or animal nature formed by combustion, weather and industry . . . even ashes from a cigarette, fireplaces and open flames, seasonal pollens, mildew, dust mites that feast on heaps of dead skin, batteries, viruses, human and animal refuse (like skin, hair, dandruff, nails, and scales of flesh). A ball of pelusa can compromise your respiratory tracts, the skin and the mucus (pelusitis, rhinitis, sinusitis, bronchitis, asthma, eczema, conjunctivitis, cold, influenza, pneumonia) . . . the flow of air spreads it all throughout the house. Study the quantities of pelusa that shift from one place to another throughout the house, and the channels they take (Important: record every draft that goes through the house, and draw a map of the air currents if possible). Then color the tiles according to the chromatic method: shade most tread-upon tiles dark red (for example: in front of the bathroom mirror, near the toilet, in front of the stove, around the dining table), and then shade the tiles that are only rarely tread upon a lighter pink. Then you'll have a floor painted in different shades . . . Define the shades from bright red to light pink: every ten centimeters shift to a lighter tone . . . Live in the space as if we were all behind a glass wall, inside a glass bottle. Let nothing escape your eye.

I'm creating order . . . a lattice of classifications and differences.

Look how our thoughts are structured: classify, order, catalog, register, inventory, taxonomize, record, select, remove and add, sketch, list, archive, name, regroup . . . find the interstitial blank that separates each one from the others . . . artificially divide the real through a process of scrupulous classification.

Anselmo put down the *Brief essay on domestic taxonomy* and shut everything back inside the little leather suitcase. He took the loan card the man had filled out and marked the due date in his calendar. He also wrote down the name of Professor Francesca Chiusaroli and in parentheses, "John Wilkins."

At a quarter to two he heard his colleagues stamp their time cards.

"Have a nice lunch," they said in unison from outside the door. But Anselmo didn't respond.

Fifteen minutes later he left the library carrying the little leather suitcase. It was a gray day, with a low, humid sky. On a whim he sat down on a bench in front of a fountain in the city garden to watch the jets of water shoot out from the mouths of the two griffins with outspread wings. He set his hat on his lap and smoothed his hair back with his hand. He spent a moment contemplating a small Madonna perched in a niche high on the wall, with ivy cascading down. Then he got up, plucked two hairs from his nose and went back to the square. He went into a bar and ordered a sandwich and tonic water with three slices of lemon. The bartender finished washing the glasses behind the counter, dried his hands, and wrapped Anselmo's sandwich in a paper towel.

"So," said the bartender, showing his large teeth. "How are you doing?"

"All right," Anselmo replied, and went to sit at a table near the window.

Perhaps this man would understand if he told him he was tired of the life he led, of feeling himself age in front of a computer screen, of never speaking with anyone. When he finished eating he ordered a coffee and lingered at the table to read the newspaper. Finally he paid the bill, strolled the city streets a bit, and at four-thirty went back to the library. He wondered why he'd brought that man's suitcase with him but had no idea why. He cataloged ten books of no importance. Then, when he picked up *On Murder Considered as one of the Fine Arts* by De Quincey, he thought how nice it would be if he could poison the two lazy ladies that he could now hear chatting in the reading room with arsenic. He had never contemplated this before. He knew that he would never do it, but it pleased him to think he could become a killer, if he truly wanted to. He pushed back his chair and opened his office door. He watched the two women speaking for a moment and contemplated their deaths by poison, imagined them writhing on the earth and spitting out a liquid like detergent. He greeted them with a malicious grin. They stared at him, not understanding. Then they burst out laughing. Anselmo slammed the door, burrowed back into his office, and didn't come out until closing. At a quarter past seven he left to take the bus home. The rather mild winter had slipped away, and now fields carpeted with grain announced the spring he could feel in the air. High temperatures only reinvigorated the dust. It became more visible, more corporeal and oppressing.

When he got home and opened the door he saw Elena at the window. She was wearing a plush cotton bathrobe printed with yellow and white daisies, with an oval neckline. She was wearing colored terry cloth slippers with short socks, her legs nude and her hair held back by a butterfly clip. Her eyes looked shiny and lost. Anselmo knew right away that she was drowning in one of her binges.

"What are you looking at?"

"Nothing, the cars."

"The cars?"

"I like to watch the cars stop at the stop sign."

Anselmo had nothing to say. He picked up the vodka bottle, just to confirm she'd almost finished it. Then he shut himself away in his study. She poured another half-glass and hid the bottle in the cupboard. A half-hour later she got it back out and poured herself another half-glass. This time she set the bottle on the table and went back to the window. She blew on the window and drew a round little face with a big smile curling upward in the fog.

Shut away in his study, Anselmo sat over a white sheet of paper, his elbows propped on the table and his eyes staring at the tip of his pen.

Esteemed Adrián Bravi,

As I'm sure you're already aware, you forgot your little leather suitcase when you borrowed the Hudson volume this morning. One of my coworkers found it on a chair. We are keeping it for you in the back office.

I want to take this opportunity to resume the conversation we started this morning about dust. You noticed, in one glance, the thin lining of dust on the library tables, and your observation meant a lot to me. I thought I'd finally met someone I could talk to. Then, if the idea of pelusa exists, with all the discomforts it creates, it means that we have, you might say, the ability to expose it at any moment. We can't ignore this ability, even if we know what causes pelusa. Pelusa is stronger than me. I can't close my eyes and ignore it. I ask myself: which can't I do without, cleaning or not cleaning? This dilemma assaults me every day. It seems I lose either way, whether I clean or not. Then I prefer to lose with a clean home. Someone, however, might tell me he feels these things ruin his life. And yet, I ask myself, what is there for him in that? If he can't feel he's keeping his home clean, then he wouldn't be able to feel anything at all. Don't you think so?

Feel free to contact me directly at home, if you prefer not to come to the library. I say this because some people can't stand my coworkers and want to avoid that place. My address is below.

Cordially,

Anselmo del Vescovo

He finished writing the letter and left his study. Elena was still near the window.

"Elena, you know, sooner or later I should go to Argentina," Anselmo said. "Today I met a very striking Argentine man. It seems Argentines are a very clean people, and simply can't stand dust. They don't even take off their hats for fear of dust. And they're obsessed with classifying everything. It seems like rigor and cleanliness are fundamental priorities for them."

Elena listened distractedly. She went on blowing on the glass, then drawing little round faces with curling smiles in the fog with her finger.

"Go on, keep dirtying up the window. As long as I'm the one that cleans it, right?"

"It's a nice night outside."

"Don't you get tired of standing right there all the time?"

"I like it."

"And have you eaten?"

"Why, what time is it?"

"Nine."

"I didn't make anything, I'm so sorry," she said, rubbing her eyes and stepping back from the window. She lost her balance for a moment, then managed to grab onto a chair.

"Come on, let me help you. You should go to bed."

Anselmo took her arm and led her into the bedroom.

"Do you love me?" Her face had turned pale and tender.

"Yes, I love you. Now calm down and sleep." He took off her shoes and laid her down on the bed.

"Oh, Anselmo! Remember when we met? . . . Do you remember?"

"Sure, I remember everything. Now try to relax and sleep off your drinking. Want to wash your face with cold water?"

"Cold water! No . . . just leave me here. Make yourself something to eat."

Anselmo stooped down and kissed her forehead. Her skin was warm and beaded with sweat. Her hair smelled sweetly of conditioner. He stroked it with his finger.

"I love you, Anselmo," she said with her eyes closed.

"You're tired. Now go to sleep."

By then more than thirty days had passed since Anselmo had mailed his letter to that stranger Adrián Bravi, and he still had heard nothing back. The man hadn't come back to return the book he borrowed, or to retrieve his suitcase. He started to think those essays on nature and the classification of dust must not have been very important to Bravi. Still he didn't rule out the possibility that something had happened to him or that he'd suddenly had to return to Argentina. He finally came to the conclusion that he needed to go in person to the address written on the loan card, to give the stranger his suitcase and talk to him a bit about the sheets he'd read from it.

It was late afternoon. Anselmo could hear his coworkers chatting through his office door. He wasn't willing to consider the day over without first writing a message to his friend.

Dear Paolo,

There are no precise rules for how to take off a wool sweater or a dirty sock, but you still ought to follow certain steps, certain behavioral norms, you might say. My wife, for example, is completely oblivious to wasting clothing or skin. Some people see no problem with leaving the window open, even if there's a sandy breeze or an ambush of gnats waiting outside the window. People like this have no idea how much damage they do, and how they force others to suffer the consequences. Just try to take off a cotton T-shirt in backlight, or try to beat a blanket in a room lit by natural light, or blow on the dandruff that's fallen like fresh snow on the pages of an open book or on the Catinari cultural commissioner's jacket. Then yes, you'll understand that there's an absolute nothingness that rules over us, and leaves us defenseless. Paolo, why does no one notice pelusa? Why can't we describe it? Why must it always torment us?

I want to pit water and darkness against earth and light.

He sent this email to the usual address. After a few seconds it came back: *The following addresses had permanent fatal errors . . . Host unknown . . .* He turned off the computer and shot out of his chair. He wanted to resolve the matter of the suitcase as soon as possible. He copied the address from the loan card onto a slip of paper and put on his hat. He stamped his time card an hour before closing and told his colleagues he needed to leave early. He hurried down the stairs and went out into the weak light of the street. As he walked he shifted the suitcase from one hand to the other and thought of that strange *Brief essay on domestic taxonomy*.

He crossed the main square and kept going until he reached the city gate. Then he took a narrow alley into the old Jewish ghetto and asked a barber where Via dei Marini was. It was easy to find. It was a little lane about fifty meters long that climbed up a stone staircase. He rang the bell at number 31 and waited, looking up to a high window. A middle-aged man with sleepy eyes opened the door. He had an unbuttoned shirt, a large stomach, and a face cut in two by a black mustache. Anselmo hadn't expected to find himself in front of anyone other than the man he'd met in the library. He looked the man up and down, disoriented for a moment.

"Now what do you want?" the man asked, rubbing his belly in a circle.

"I'm looking for Mr. Adrián Bravi," said Anselmo, taking his hand out of his coat pocket.

"There's no Adrián Bravi here."

"But they gave me this address."

"They must be mistaken, what do you want me to tell you? I don't know anyone by that name."

"Are you sure?"

"Positive."

"Strange."

"Ah, I understand," said the man with a sneer. "Any chance this is another social security check and you want me to think you're looking for someone? Anyway, I'm at home, I'm sick. My stomach is killing me. I have the right to have a stomachache, don't I?"

Anselmo looked at the man's stomach and the dark circles under his eyes. He had no doubt this man had a stomachache. The man stepped aside to let Anselmo in, but he stayed on the doorstep.

"Go on, go on," he said. "Are you a doctor?"

"No, I'm not a doctor. I'm a librarian."

"A librarian? And what do you want?" he asked, this time showing his teeth, which were stained with a visible crust of nicotine.

"I'm just looking for this Adrián Bravi, but apparently there's been a mistake."

"I've already told you, no Adrián Bravi lives here."

Anselmo felt his chance of speaking with the owner of that little leather suitcase slipping further and further away. He tried to focus on the objects near the entrance: an unstable wood table, an ashtray full of chewing gum, a dirty floor, and an old pink cabinet. A nauseating stuffy smell hung over everything.

"So, tell me," repeated the pale, bulging-eyed man, who kept rubbing his stomach. "Is this some kind of trap? I know you guys from social security play these little games. Anyhow, look, I'm here with a stomach that's killing me."

"No, I didn't come here to check anything. I'm only looking for the owner of this little suitcase that was forgotten in the library."

"Show me," said the sick man, trying to pull the little suitcase out of Anselmo's hands.

"But . . . what are you doing?"

"Show me, I said."

"It's not yours."

"They gave you this address?"

"Yes, but obviously it was a mistake."

"No, here it's only me, Riccardo Deriu. I've lived here for two years. I pay my rent and taxes."

"Congratulations, Mr. Deriu, but that's not why I'm here."

"I know, you can't even get sick in peace because suddenly all the inspectors swoop in on you. I bet my boss told you: 'Go check in on him. See if he's at home or out on the town.'"

"But I'm not an inspector. Anyway, with things how they are, I just want to say I'm sorry to bother you and I'll be off."

"Oh, it's no bother. But, since you aren't from welfare, sit down and have a little drink with me," he said, pointing to a stool in the center of the room under a chandelier made of a large ball of diaphanous paper. The man opened the old pink cabinet and took out a bottle of red wine and two glasses. He set them on the table, pulled out a chair that was missing a leg and sat down gingerly, taking care to balance out the missing leg. He filled the glasses with wine and said, "To our health!"

"If your stomach hurts, you should take care of yourself."

"Take care of myself? Baloney. To stomachaches," the man said, emptying the glass in one gulp. "And tell me, what's your name?"

"Anselmo."

"Anselmo," the man repeated, stressing every syllable. "Anselmo What?"

"Del Vescovo."

"Del Vescovo! Like a bishop? But what kind of last name is that? Don't make me laugh. Whatever, I don't care one bit. Too bad for you. So, Bishop, you're looking for someone who has this address? That makes me curious, you know?"

"Are you Argentine, by any chance?" Anselmo asked, even though the man had no foreign accent.

"Why, do you have something against Argentines?"

"The person I'm looking for is Argentine."

"Nope. No Argentine in me at all. I'm Sardinian, if you really want to know. But are you sure you're not from social security?"

"I already told you, I'm not from social security. I'm a librarian."

"Now let's have another little glass, what do you say?"

"I'm fine right now."

"Well, from the look of it you wouldn't think so," he laughed, pressing on his stomach. "So you're a librarian."

"Uh, yeah."

"And is that boring?"

"Well, sometimes. It depends. And what do you do?"

"I'm a warehouseman."

"Oh, interesting."

"Are you pulling my leg?"

"I wanted to ask you something else. By any chance have you received a letter I sent about a month ago?"

"You? To me?"

"I sent it to Adrián Bravi, but I addressed it here, to 31 Via dei Marini."

The man got up from his broken chair clumsily. He got a letter out of the old pink cabinet and carefully sat back down. "This one?" he asked, waving the letter.

"Yes, that one. But it wasn't for you."

"Whatever." The man pulled up the hem of his pants and with pained expression added, "I even have swollen ankles, you see? That job is ruining me, let me tell you, just in case you're a social security inspector."

"What do I have to do to make you believe I'm not from social security?"

"Well, you don't even look like one, but then you can't trust anyone these days. Know what I mean?"

"Of course."

"Well, if you're not checking on me, take this letter back." He slid it across the table. He leaned back in his chair, lit a cigarette, and said, "I'm curious to know what's inside that little suitcase."

"Nothing in particular."

"You looked inside it?"

"I had to, for security reasons. But when I saw it was only papers and notes, I closed it."

"Clearly you're an honest person, but I bet if you'd found something interesting your honesty would've gone off to fuck itself."

"How could I let that happen?"

"I'd let it happen, I'd let it happen," said the man, hugging his stomach with both hands. "And do you know why I'd let it happen? Because it's not your job to be honest, not mine, not anybody's. Trusting an honest man is like trusting a happy man. It's very risky." He emptied the glass and kept his hand on his stomach, which now moved up and down with the rhythm of his breathing.

Anselmo took advantage of this pause to look around. The

old wallpaper was faded, flecked with dark humidity stains. The front door, which gave out onto the alley, was painted pastel green with black steps below. In the corners of the floor sat old orange peels, crumpled cigarette packs, butts, and empty beer bottles from who knows when. On the table where the man left Anselmo's letter lay *La settimana enigmistica* and a local newspaper open to the sports page.

"Well," said Anselmo, rising from the stool, "I should go home. If by chance you learn something about the existence of a certain Adrián Bravi tell him we have his little suitcase in the city library." The man also got up and leaned his chair against the table very naturally, showing no sign that it was missing one leg.

"I will," he said. "And you, remember that I'm sick and I can't leave my house for a week. Also say that the family doctor prescribed me full bed rest until Monday. I'm telling you in case you have to report back to some welfare inspectors."

"Don't worry. I'll tell the inspectors you were resting in bed, as you should be."

"Thank you so much. You must be a great librarian."

"Good evening, and excuse me for bothering you."

Anselmo turned and left that small, awful-smelling house. He went back down the stairs of Via dei Marini, walked back through the Jewish ghetto, and returned home. Low, thick clouds hung over the streets. Others would've found that weather depressing, but not Anselmo, who loved rain, snow, and anything else that blocked the sunlight. He walked with a measured step, only occasionally seeing someone else. He stopped for no reason, cleaned his glasses with a handkerchief, then returned to his path hugging the city walls, mechanically touching his folder with the documents and the little suitcase that he shifted from one hand to the other.

When he arrived home, he found his wife sitting on the couch with her legs crossed and head leaned back.

"Are you okay?" he said, taking off his shoes.

"Yes, I just have a little headache. I took some valerians and half an acetaminophen."

"Why do you get headaches so often?"

"I don't know. It must be the weather."

"Maybe you should pay more attention to what you eat, or at least what you drink."

"Maybe. In the meantime the vacuum is on the table." She was in no mood to talk and neither was he.

Anselmo took off his coat and pants. Elena's illness made him want to do a bit of cleaning. He took a sponge mop and began cleaning the floor. Minerals, seed, pollen, insects, insect excrement, mold, lichens, bacteria, sand brought in by the wind, bits of cheese, threads tangled with hair and wool fibers that swayed at the slightest gust of air like dust bunnies or lay hidden for months, years, centuries, in the inaccessible corners between the wall and the leg of an old cabinet, under the refrigerator, on top of the wardrobe. Worm-eaten morsels of bread, coffee grounds, sugar, cotton, skin. He felt submerged in a crowd of these elements, and no longer knew how to extricate himself from that labyrinth, like trying to pull the thoughts out of his head. When he finished cleaning, he took off all his clothes on the balcony and shook them out vigorously, one at a time. Then he stepped into the shower. The water slid down his hair, dragging all the dirt on his body toward the drain.

"You have red cheeks," Elena said when she saw her husband wrapped in a green dressing gown, coming out of the bathroom, which was still full of steam. "That means you're happy."

Anselmo touched his cheeks without saying anything. He turned on the stereo and listened to the same Brahms andante seven times while he ate.

He jolted awake at five the next morning, thinking of the nightly contamination. He had dreamed that one of his coworkers was hiding under the desk in his office, masturbating.

He managed to go back to sleep. He got up abruptly, put on his glasses, went to make coffee, and started cleaning the house. He moved the refrigerator, washing machine, and two cabinets. He cleaned the floor with vinegar to remove the stains, wiped it with a rag soaked in lemon detergent, and put things back. Then he took a quick shower, and left for work at seven-thirty.

Elena got up when she heard him close the door. She went to the window and watched her husband walk briskly to the bus stop. She waited to watch him get on the bus. Then she went back to bed, where she spent more than an hour curled up in a ball with her knees at her chest.

At nine in the morning, the doorbell rang. Elena stood near the stove watching the coffee gurgle. She listened distractedly to a song on the radio and did not answer it right away. She looked around and tried to smooth her hair.

"Who are you?" she said, buttoning her robe to the top button.

"I need to deliver something to Mr. Anselmo Del Vescovo."

"One moment."

When Elena opened the door she found a corpulent man, wrapped in an anorak with an upturned collar, wearing checkered pants, and holding an extinguished cigarette in his hand. He was a bit rotund, with a black mustache that covered his upper lip.

"Hello, ma'am," the man said. "Yesterday your husband, I suppose, came to my home and forgot this letter. I wanted to give it back to him, since it isn't for me." He half-closed his eyes as he spoke, as if he were searching for the words.

"Okay, but he didn't say anything to me about it."

"It's not important . . . Watch out!" he burst out, pointing to the coffee machine that was boiling over the bluish flame. Elena hurried over and turned off the gas. "Anyway, it isn't addressed to me, even though it has my address. And since I saw your husband, I've been thinking . . ."

"Please, have a seat. Do you want a coffee? It's already made."

The man walked into the apartment, which smelled of lemon detergent. It was so clean it was like a mirror. He took off his jacket, then lost his balance for a moment as he was getting ready to sit down. When he regained his balance, he smiled and sat down.

"I'd love to, but then I'll need to go right away because the welfare inspectors might come to check."

"Are you sick?"

"Yes, my stomach is killing me."

"And what did the doctor say?"

"That it's nothing, there's just something out of balance, that's all. I wondered, since your husband works for social security, if they have doctors there that understand gastritis or stuff like that."

"My husband doesn't work for social security."

"No? Where does he work?"

"He works at the library."

"Never mind then, I must be confused."

She set the sugar and two cups of coffee on the table.

"And you, what do you do?" Elena asked while she was stirring the sugar into her coffee.

"I'm a warehouse chief. It's a lot of responsibility, you know? I have to be ready for every request. I mean, I'm the first and the last link in the chain."

"I can imagine."

The man looked at her for a moment and Elena noticed that, for the first time in a long time, a man's eyes were lingering on her. The man finished his coffee, took a handkerchief out of his pocket, and meticulously cleaned his mustache.

"That was a great coffee," he finally said. "Made by hands like yours, it had to be good."

She didn't answer, and kept her hands on the table, feeling a certain embarrassment. Then she got up, collected both cups, and set them in the sink.

"Well," the man said getting up from the chair. "I'll stop bothering you."

"Oh, you're not bothering me at all."

"I don't trust social security inspectors. When one has a job with a lot of responsibility like mine, they're always lurking. They start doing inspections at ten, and if they don't find me at home there'll be hell to pay."

"If you must."

"Ah, I forgot to leave you your husband's letter," he said, holding out the letter addressed to Adrián Bravi. He put his jacket back on and turned the collar up.

He opened the door and said, "I hope to see you again soon. It's been a pleasure."

The man leaned forward to get as close to Elena as possible and said in a low voice, "One day I'll make you try the coffee I make. It's not like yours, but . . ." He started down the steps, then stopped. "Ah, my name is Riccardo, Riccardo Deriu."

"I'm Elena." She stood immobile on the threshold. She looked at the address on the envelope and went back inside.

It was a sunny morning in early May, maybe the most beautiful morning yet that spring, she thought. Finally she could feel the air wrapping its warmth around her. She went to the window and looked down on the row of poplars that lined the lane below the apartment. She opened the shutters, felt a strong wind brush her face, and immediately shut them again. She was tired of Anselmo's lectures about opening the windows. Every day he warned her, "Pay attention because the poplar pollen season is starting soon."

She wondered, "Why do I have to live in this airtight box, when outside the sun is so beautiful?"

She opened the shutters again and left them wide open. How could she have indulged her husband's paranoia for two long years? She, who was born and grew up in the country, clambering over the trees with her cousins, chasing the geese across the meadow. She, who at just that time of year used to help her cousins pick artichoke and fava beans, and started looking forward to the taste of cherries. She, who now had to live in a fourth-floor apartment with the windows shut to keep out the dust. She sat on the couch, with the window open, until the doorbell rang again. She opened the door.

It was a saleswoman who'd come to deliver the vacuum cleaner. Stunned, Elena looked her up and down, and couldn't muster the nerve to tell her to come back later, when her husband would be home. The saleswoman's large lips opened and closed on a set of perfect teeth beneath a pointed nose, framed by voluminous hair that moved when she did, brushing her shoulders. Her curves would've intimidated anyone. When the saleswoman took off her coat, Elena felt even more weak and fragile in front of her, like a delicate little figurine, or even a child. But what struck her even more was this woman's ease and self-certainty, two qualities she'd always envied in women that knew how to wear their own femininity. The saleswoman showed her how to use the vacuum, how to swap out the filters, how to change the parts, how to put it together and clean the couch or the mattress. She watched Elena almost tenderly. She could see Elena was a fragile woman, so she accentuated her methods of persuasion and her shameless way of showing off her beauty.

"You won't regret it. Now you'll be able to clean quickly and thoroughly."

Finally, the woman put all the accessories back in the box and let Elena see for herself how easy it was to manage. She flicked the switch and slid the nozzle back and forth on the floor. This convinced her. She went to get her husband's checkbook. She signed the check, tore it out, and gave it to the saleswoman. She thought she'd never seen a woman so beautiful and sure of herself. She walked her down to the ground floor and said a warm goodbye. She went back into the apartment, took the calendar and drew a large X on the second Friday in May. Under it she wrote *Big Day*.

Anselmo came straight home after work. He took off his shoes on the doorstep and put on the slippers Elena brought him. Every day for two years they'd performed that ritual, always exactly the same way. This time, however, he noticed his wife's face was friendlier, more cordial than usual. She smiled more broadly and cleaned his shoes more purposefully.

As much as Elena smiled, as much as she wanted to seem kind, she was anxious that the vacuum cleaner story would send her plummeting back down that dark hole she filled with vodka every night. She began to feel anguish at having to tell her husband that she'd torn out one of his checks to buy a vacuum cleaner without consulting him. She asked him how his day at work had been, but he didn't answer.

"So, do you have anything to say to me?"

"What do you want me to say? If I don't clean this house myself, no one does!" Anselmo answered.

He left his somewhat disconcerted wife and went to shut himself away in his study. He got the detergent from the cabinet and poured a good amount on his desk. Then he took a piece of paper and cleaned the surface four or five times. He went back over the edge of the chair, the corner of a painting, the dust stuck to his computer screen. Finally he turned on his computer and wrote:

Paolo,

I dust and I dust. I'm never adding anything, just taking it away. But somehow the more I take away, the more there is to take away. I see all these things looking faded, and I do nothing but clean to restore their color in the light. A particle that flits about, lost in the air, sends me into a rage. Two hairs twisted together on the ground destroy me. A sneeze that explodes from my mouth horrifies me, the unthinkable grime that sticks to the sole of my shoes is chasing me . . . and there's pelusa, pelusa, pelusa, pelusa everywhere. How long will we have to tolerate pelusa?

When he came out of his study a half-hour later, Elena threw her arms around his neck and kissed him.

"Why can't we forget everything and start over, Anselmo?" she said.

Anselmo interrogated her with his eyes. He couldn't understand what she wanted from him. In that moment, however, he knew that everything was a mistake, all of this, his childhood, his marriage, his job, his entire way of being and perceiving things. It had all turned out completely wrong.

"Come with me, Anselmo, I want to surprise you. But first you have to close your eyes."

"I don't feel like playing games right now. Show me what you need to show me."

Elena took his hand and showed him the vacuum cleaner. Leaning against the wall, it looked like a little spaceship, impeccable, infallible, ready to suck all the dust of the world back inside. But unfortunately she didn't know that, despite the modern design and ultra-light brushes, this machine would torment him, rather than lighten his burden of cleaning.

"Did you already pay for it?"

"Look how beautiful it is," she said, showing him a page of the manual. "It can capture ninety-nine point ninety-seven percent of particles larger than zero point zero-zero-zero-three millimeters." She finished reading and rested a knowing look on him, caressing his hair sweetly. She didn't understand, however, that it was just that fraction of a millimeter the vacuum cleaner couldn't capture that would send Anselmo into a rage.

"You can't even see further than your own nose."

"What do you mean? I did it for you." Elena's face contracted suddenly.

"No, you didn't do it for me. You did it for yourself. And you already paid for it?"

"Yes, I signed a check."

"You need to learn to take care of your own things."

"Don't you understand that you are one of my own things, Anselmo?"

"Then you should do what I say. I've told you a hundred times that machines like this don't solve the problem of cleaning. All they do is blow the dust through the air, move it from one place to another and this way and that way, and make you think you've cleaned it. I've always warned you about miracle solutions like this. What can clean a house better than a damp cloth? But you've never cared about that anyway, so why are you trying to impose new methods on me?"

He got a wet cloth and started cleaning the windows. Some of them were still smudged from the past few days' rain. Elena sat at the kitchen table, reading one of the women's magazines she flipped through before bed. Every so often her eyes fell on the vacuum cleaner leaning against the wall. If only her husband could get over his problem with dust! Deep down, however, she hadn't truly believed that this gadget could be her way out. She ate alone, washed the dishes, and then went into the bedroom.

When he finished cleaning the windows, Anselmo went over the shelves again. He took a shower and went to bed himself.

In the middle of the night, Elena began crying in her sleep, with a light rustle that grew louder and louder. Anselmo got up, turned on the lamp on the nightstand and, out of fear that she would start kicking again, shook her arm to wake her up.

"Were you dreaming?"

"Me? No."

"You weren't?"

"I don't remember."

"You were crying like a lunatic."

Anselmo turned off the light, rolled over to the other side and fell asleep again. Elena curled up again and closed her eyes.

The next morning Anselmo got up right away to resume his cleaning where he'd left off the night before. He took a row of books out of his bookcase and cleaned the wooden shelf with a special beeswax-based cleanser. He put the books back and did the same for the other eighteen shelves. He shook his clothes out on the balcony, then took a hot shower. At seven-thirty he left to catch the bus. It was Saturday morning and the bus was full of people headed to the market in the central square, just like every Saturday. He hated people who went to the market. Even the lazy ladies went shopping there. They stamped their time cards and then came up with some implausible excuse for why they had to go out for thirty or forty minutes. Only four or five people came in that morning. Recently, Anselmo had been so inhospitable that even schoolchildren had deserted the library. He discouraged reading, wouldn't lend them more than one book at a time, and barred them from using the photocopier. He bought books that were further and further afield from patrons' requests.

Paolo,

Have you ever thought how life might be if everything were slowly growing larger and larger before our eyes? And if we became smaller and smaller until we found ourselves lost in the vast kingdom of dust, struggling to extricate ourselves from the hair, insects, and everything we can't see? Would we still have our names? How'd you like to get into a brawl with a mite?

He sent the message and after a few seconds it came back: *The following addresses had permanent fatal errors . . . Host unknown . . .*

Paolo,

Have you ever wondered how there can be so much dust in a man's navel? How does that happen? Does the navel produce the dust itself, secreting oils that blend with the fabric of our clothing?

He sent this email as well, but after a few seconds it came back with the same message as before.

At one-ten he left the library. He crossed the square, passing pieces of paper, receipts that flitted about here and there, scraps left behind from the market, and the warm tropical wind that blew the dust into your eyes. It was hot. Spring's first pollen was beginning to wander through the air and everything Anselmo saw was covered by a blanket of dust. The square, the air, the shop windows, his own skin. At one-forty he got home and opened the door. But this time his wife didn't meet him with his slippers. He called her name twice, but no one answered. He went to get them himself. The pores of his skin felt clogged with dust, his clothes felt full of dust. He couldn't take off his own clothes inside the house, or his movements would diffuse all the filth attached to the clothes.

He went into the shower, still fully clothed, and turned on the stream of water. It was pleasant to feel that beneficent liquid carry all those revolting particles away toward the pipes. When his clothes were fully soaked he took them off, peeling back the sleeves. He dried off and went into the kitchen. On the table he found a letter from Elena.

Dear Anselmo,

When I got up this morning, I called my mother to ask how she was, since I hadn't called her for a while. I said, "Hi, Mom. It's Elena." She said, "Elena who?" I knew she needed me, so I packed my suitcase in a hurry and now I'm ready to leave this house behind. On the other hand, you've made it clear over and over that I'm nothing but aggravation for you, and maybe you'd prefer to be alone. Deep down you've always seen me the way you see dust, like an intruder that's broken in from outside and occupies your living space: living room, kitchen, bathroom, etcetera. When you fight every day to drive dust out of the house, you drive me out, too. If that's not the case, call me at my mother's. I'll be there when you get back from work. This time, however, you'll have to get your slippers yourself. And if you need to clean your shoes, you'll have to do that too.

I'm sorry.

Yours,

Elena

He dropped the letter on the table. As he ate his gaze fell every so often on the vacuum cleaner that leaned against the wall. He thought of mites, imagining them as tiny balls digging in, clinging to your clothing, and grasping at your skin, feeding on flakes of skin, always growing and getting stronger. He couldn't finish what he was eating. He jumped out of his chair and plugged the vacuum cleaner into the electric socket. Then he looked at it for a long time. He was putting his health, both physical and mental, in jeopardy. He hesitated a bit longer, as it seemed destined to set off a bomb. Finally he turned it on. The machine whirred like an air turbine. Anselmo moved it back and forth like a fool. Then he stopped to check the power of the air that was blasting out from the side hole. After a few seconds he turned it off and stared, horrified, at the dust that whirled about within a ray of light through the windowpanes. He stood stunned by that glittering mass of particles that rose and fell gently, that vanished, swallowed by the shadows, and then reappeared in the light. "These particles are throwing their own little party in my house!" he shouted. He was certain the fine dust that he now saw spinning was the rest of that ninety-nine point ninety-seven percent of particles thicker than zero point zero zero zero three millimeters. He picked up the vacuum slowly but decisively, then let it fall to the ground with a boom that echoed through the whole apartment. He picked it back up and let it fall again, cracking its handle. He kicked it, bringing it outside to his balcony. He sat back down, his arms spread open wide. He couldn't feel like himself again. His jaws were so clenched with rage that his throat swelled up, his tendons tightened, and his jugular vein stood out under his skin like a trapped earthworm. Then Anselmo calmed down. He felt alone in his dust-filled home. He closed all the blinds to block out the sun's glare and started cleaning the floor with a wet cloth. He took another hot shower. That ray of light loaded with particles had been one blast.

Paolo,

What's happened to you? Help me, if you're my friend. Answer me.

He sat before his computer, not speaking, not moving, like a spider frozen still in its old web. He felt like a man who'd grown up too hastily. A long stream of saliva dribbled from his mouth, and he wiped it away with the back of his hand. *The following addresses had permanent fatal errors . . . Host unknown . . .* He went into the kitchen to make himself a coffee. He went back into his study to write again.

Four white walls, a white radiator in the middle of one of them. A ceiling white like the walls, a brown floor with geometric patterns, a light brown table with four chairs, a white fridge, a closed window, also white, a white front door with a frosted glass window above it, and a peephole one meter and sixty centimeters above the ground. A black display case with a television and a VCR, all covered with a plastic cover impermeable to dust. A couch where no one sits, made of soft black leather, with four thin chrome legs. A green sage table at the entrance and a painting of an autumn landscape with large trees and six birds that plow a field of gray clouds hanging from two nails above it. By the window a sink on top of a little white stand. Next to it, a white stove and a white dishwasher with a black radio above it. All of this is laid out in a space of twenty-four by twenty-eight tiles, each one twenty-by-twenty centimeters. The baseboard is made of light brown wood, like the table. From the window you can constantly hear noise from the street: cars, mopeds, a fishmonger, and a man who sells spring mattresses. Below this floor is the same room repeated four times, and in each one, someone like me who may do the same things I do: clean, write, go out, come in. Maybe he opens the window when it's hot. I'm hot but I leave it closed. Maybe he opens the blinds to let the light in. Instead I close them to keep it out. Our everyday lives vary in fundamental ways, according to shifts in our actions and perceptions.

Reinforce my interventions against the microcosm and safeguard the space that surrounds me.

It was almost nine in the evening. Now he could open the shutters again without worrying about the sunlight. He went to bed, but couldn't fall asleep. For two or three hours he lay stiff, fixating on the ceiling's cave-like gloom, his eyes blocked off by the darkness.

The next day he got up at four-thirty. From the kitchen window he looked out at the phalanx of poppies that lined the lane and blamed his wife for leaving him the moment those trees were starting to exude their aggravating spring fuzz. He made himself a coffee and then, still wearing his multicolored pajamas, started pulling the drawers out of the wardrobe so he could shake all the clothes out on the balcony. At seven-thirty on that sunny Sunday in May he closed all the shutters and turned on the electric lights. He spent the whole day at home, organizing everything and wiping the entire floor down with his cloth.

Paolo,

I'm waiting for this thundering symphony of particles to stop. The more I see dust, the more it empties my soul.

On Monday morning he got up at five. The idea of going to work, with everything he had to do at home, made him nervous. He couldn't leave the apartment and all its furniture alone, at the mercy of dust. At eight-oh-five he called the library and spoke with one of the lazy ladies. He told her he felt ill and couldn't come to work. He set down the phone and thought, "It doesn't seem like it takes much of a reason to stay home. Knowing them, they'd need reasons to go to work, rather." Then he went to the doctor to get a certificate.

"What do you have?" the doctor asked.

"A headache, I have a pain right here that hurts so bad I can't stand it. I need to take a few days off. I'm exhausted from work."

"Do you have vertigo?"

"Yes, all the time. I can't move."

"I'll give you twenty days of rest. That should be enough. Try to drink a lot of water and take two tablets a day," the doctor said, writing down the name of the pharmacy.

He left the office and went to the pharmacy. He had the impression everyone was looking at him strangely. He even passed the post office and then went to the store to stock up on detergent. Then he went straight home. He took off his shoes and put on his slippers. He had twenty days to get his apartment in order. He unfastened his collar and sat at his computer.

Paolo,

I'll be home for a little while, and I'm taking advantage of it to take care of some little things that need doing. But please, let's put deep thoughts aside. What could we even want to bring to light from those depths? Let's concentrate on the folds in the surface. The infinite, which has tortured so many minds, is nothing more than dust.

On Tuesday morning a postman with a tired, sweaty face, dusty jacket, and dirty shoes came up to the fourth floor to bring him a registered letter. Anselmo tried to hold it as far away from himself as he could. He went back in, closing the door immediately. He opened the envelope and unfolded the letter on the table.

Dear Anselmo,

You still haven't called me, not even once. I won't call you, even if I'm the one who left. I prefer to write you and I'm sending this letter first thing tomorrow morning, so you can read it right away. I can't imagine how you interpreted my leaving you (I'm trying to use the words you might be using right now, even though I don't see it as leaving you at all). I've needed to escape for some time. I can't forget all the times I've suffocated my anxiety and fears with crying. With you I'm always wrong, even the way I clean is wrong. Anyway, now I'm here with my mother and I don't know how long I'll stay with her. I expect you to call me or write me just two words, at least to know how I am.

Hugs.

Yours,

Elena

He cleaned the house all day without a break. He got up very early again the next day to get back to cleaning. He had specific plans and it wasn't enough for things to *look* clean. He had to be sure there wasn't a single grain of dust, not even under the fridge or the wardrobe. So he decided it was fundamentally important to lay out a work plan. And that entire day, from when he got up until he went to bed, he did nothing but clean. It would strain his imagination to try to separate morning from afternoon and afternoon from evening. A boiled egg, pasta with oil, or a slice of bread with olive spread were his only ways of breaking up the day and taking a break from cleaning for a few minutes.

Paolo,

I'm afraid . . . There's so much of it here! I wish so badly that I could turn my life around!

At nine on Wednesday morning the doorbell rang. Through the peephole he saw Riccardo Deriu's face, distorted by the lens. He opened it right away, hoping this man had come to bring him some news of Adrián Bravi, now when he needed more than ever to speak with someone who understood him. The man stepped over the threshold and looked at Anselmo, who stood with his sleeves rolled up, holding a bottle of detergent and a bucket of water.

"Are you home alone?" asked the man, who didn't expect to see Anselmo at all.

"I think so," he answered, still holding the cloth, letting it drip into the bucket.

"And you're not working today?"

"No, I'm sick."

"So are you waiting for the social security inspectors?"

"Of course."

"Well, they don't usually come before ten, but sometimes they play little games."

"I'm not worried."

"And your wife, is she here?"

"She left me, if you want to know. She went to her mother's."

"Oh, wow."

"Right. By chance, have you heard from that Adrián Bravi?"

"I don't know who he is."

"Okay. Now I have to go. The social security inspectors could come at any moment, and I have to be ready."

"Yes, it's good to be ready."

"Well, then, goodbye."

When the man went away, Anselmo went back to cleaning the floor over and over again, especially the tiles that intruder had trampled at the entrance. He felt dirty, tired, aged. It was as if he had just become aware of all that had happened to him. Everything had gone horribly wrong. Anselmo took a hot shower. His shoulders slumped. He opened the kitchen window. Outside there was a beautiful blue sky. A breeze from the sea ruffled the leaves and spread pollen from the poppies all along the street. Beyond the trees he could see the intersection where he usually waited for the bus. He closed the blinds and the window and started cleaning again. That evening he stretched out on the wet floor, took a long breath, and then lay there, looking at the tiles around him. Noise from the street woke him up, feeling stiff all over. After coffee with milk and five whole-wheat biscuits with marmalade he regained his strength. That morning the phone rang several times. Anselmo just looked at it, uncertain.

"I'll answer it some other time. Right now I don't feel like it," he thought, pleased with himself.

He couldn't keep up with the dust. He cleaned a room and

saw that it was dirty again the next day. It was as if there were ghosts taunting him, dropping dust from the ceiling. "If only I could be everywhere at once!" he thought. Later the doorbell rang again, but he preferred not to answer.

"Is anyone there?" a slightly hoarse voice called from the other side of the door. It could be the woman from the third floor who went out to walk her little mutt every morning.

Only crazy people talk to themselves, he thought. And he liked to revel in the madness of others, so he stayed silent himself.

One evening he could hear his neighbors chatting on the landing outside his door. He recognized their voices, but couldn't make out what they were saying. The doorbell rang three times but Anselmo stayed silent. He didn't understand what these people, who never greeted him in the street or on the stairs, could want from him.

"I'll answer them some other time. Now I don't feel like it."

Someone knocked on the door loudly, with a closed fist.

"Open this door, we have to talk to you!" It was a furious, jarring voice.

Then he heard all of them climbing the stairs together. Anselmo went into the bathroom, took the anti-limescale fluid and began cleaning the toilet and bidet. He felt weak, disarmed and helpless like dust. A hot shower relaxed him and gave him the strength to take all the wool sweaters that were folded in his wardrobe out onto the balcony. He did the same thing with the socks and his wife's plush cotton bathrobe, which had especially annoyed him.

Paolo

What is happening?

The following addresses had permanent fatal errors . . . Host unknown . . . He squared his shoulders and kept writing.

You're wrong, Paolo. That message wasn't a mistake. The fatal error is life.

On the fifteenth day of his illness the bell rang twice. But Anselmo sat silently on the floor, undisturbed. He'd finished wiping the room down with the wet cloth and now he was resting with his shoulders leaning against the wall.

"Open up! It's me."

The doorbell's incessant metallic sound annoyed him. He got up, turned off the light, and sat back down on the floor, his arm still lying on the bucket of water.

"Open the door!" This time it was a deep male voice. He couldn't recognize it.

"Come on, open up, Anselmo. It's me."

A key tried to fit into the keyhole, but Anselmo blocked it by inserting another key from the other side.

"Please, Anselmo, open the door. I want to talk to you."

He took the rag from the bucket, wrung it out a bit, and began to clean around him, without moving from that position. He watched with interest the little circles his hand made on the floor.

"Open the door!" the man's voice went on, insistent.

"Anselmo!"

Everything around him seemed incomprehensible. It felt like dust was chasing him, and he was becoming dust himself. With every movement, a part of him seemed to crumble. He was about to get up to take a shower.

"Open the door!"

"We'll have to break it down!"

"Please!"

Anselmo got up slowly, dropped his rag in the water, picked up the bucket and with his other hand turned the key twice. Just opening the door ought to shut up those incessant voices. He immediately felt the lock click and the door open toward the inside.

"Anselmo!" Elena cried when she saw her husband.

A traffic cop, the neighbors, his wife, and cousin all stood on the landing looking at Anselmo, who stood motionless on the threshold.

"What is this?" he asked, confused, not understanding.

"Why wouldn't you open the door?" the traffic cop asked in a menacing tone.

"What's wrong?" echoed the woman who had hung back on the third floor.

Anselmo didn't know how to respond. He thought with horror that now all those people were about to invade his house with their dirty shoes befouling the floor. Just the thought made him feel like he was suffocating. He set the bucket down on the ground and peered silently at these people who kept asking him things he could not answer. Then he abruptly slammed the door and turned the key, making all those voices fall silent. He rushed to the bathroom to take a shower. The hot water ran over his body like a blessing. When he left the bathroom he looked through the peephole and let out a sigh of relief. There was no one left on the doorstep. He was alone again. He took the rag from the water bucket, wrung it out a bit, and continued cleaning the floor glazed with dust.

At three in the morning he woke with a start. He felt as if he were searching for something in the dark. The alarm clock's hand announced the seconds, one after another. He picked up his alarm clock and took out the battery. The silence grew even denser, and still it seemed like he was hearing the sound of rain or snow, and hearing it incessantly. He got up very carefully and stayed right in the middle of the room. Now the rustle of flakes falling slowly from the ceiling was even sharper. It was the first time in his life that he heard the sound of dust: a light drizzle of dust fell from above to settle on the surface of things. Anselmo screamed loudly, then remained silent, and again listened attentively. He covered his ears with both hands. When he uncovered them the sound was just as incessant as before. He went into the kitchen and turned on the radio, but knew he was only deluding himself. And how he wished in that moment he could become a fish, glide under the water, and never again have anything to do with the filth of the air, its stockpile of particles or its revolting little creatures. He shut himself away in the bathroom and stayed under the shower stream for a half-hour. He put on clean pajamas with vertical stripes, his glasses, and slippers. Then when he turned out the light in his study he saw, horrified, on his desk, a thin layer of dust that covered the books, the computer, the edge of the shelves. He went into the kitchen and saw that even there, on the fridge's metal surface, was a thin layer of dust. Everywhere, on every last thing, there was a thin layer of dust.

He took off his glasses, turned off the lights and the radio, and listened again to the incessant sound of dust. He opened the window that faced the long phalanx of poppies that had been spreading their fuzz into the air for several weeks now. He breathed in that filthy air until it filled his lungs. Then he emptied them, then filled them again. His skin was transformed into an immense battlefield of micro-organisms, white blood cells that were swallowed up between them, bacteria that get tangled up in an atrocious battle, acrobatic germs that climb through your hair, as every little microscopic creature breaks in to take your body for its own. The overwhelming nothingness of those beings suffocated him. He rushed to open the windows in the bedroom, bathroom, and study. He dropped his free hand into the air currents that blew in and out of every opening, that ebbed and flowed through every corner of the house that had been seized from him. He opened the wardrobe, the cabinet, the fridge, the dishwasher, the washing machine, all the drawers, all the doors. He picked up his glasses and hurled them against the wall. Then he went over to the balcony.

He felt like the emptiest being in the world: without a home, without a body, without words. Life was getting rid of him in a hurry. He panted for breath, turned up the collar of his vertical-striped pajamas, looked into the void, and slowly let himself fall over the railing, like a mite that's torn from a leaf and falls onto an unfamiliar street. It was cold, despite the spring breeze, and the chill was imbued with the nauseating odor of asphalt. Anselmo looked around and tried to roll over, but his body wouldn't let him. He heard a can rolling down the street and knew exactly where he was. He opened and shut his eyes several times. He lay motionless on the ground until the first morning breeze rustled the trees and bushes, carrying away everything night had laid to rest on the pavement.

Born in Buenos Aires in 1963, Adrián Bravi moved to Italy in the late 1980s and, after studying philosophy and working as a librarian, began to publish fiction in the late 1990s. He is the author of several novels, a children's book, and numerous articles and stories. His writing has been translated into French, English, and Spanish.

Patience Haggin is a journalist and translator. She graduated from Princeton University and studied translation in Italy as a Fulbright Scholar.

MICHAL AJVAZ, *The Golden Age.*
The Other City.

PIERRE ALBERT-BIROT, *Grabinoulor.*

YUZ ALESHKOVSKY, *Kangaroo.*

FELIPE ALFAU, *Chromos.*
Locos.

JOE AMATO, *Samuel Taylor's Last Night.*

IVAN ÂNGELO, *The Celebration.*
The Tower of Glass.

ANTÓNIO LOBO ANTUNES, *Knowledge of Hell.*
The Splendor of Portugal.

ALAIN ARIAS-MISSON, *Theatre of Incest.*

JOHN ASHBERY & JAMES SCHUYLER, *A Nest of Ninnies.*

ROBERT ASHLEY, *Perfect Lives.*

GABRIELA AVIGUR-ROTEM, *Heatwave and Crazy Birds.*

DJUNA BARNES, *Ladies Almanack.*
Ryder.

JOHN BARTH, *Letters.*
Sabbatical.

DONALD BARTHELME, *The King.*
Paradise.

SVETISLAV BASARA, *Chinese Letter.*

MIQUEL BAUÇÀ, *The Siege in the Room.*

RENÉ BELLETTO, *Dying.*

MAREK BIENCZYK, *Transparency.*

ANDREI BITOV, *Pushkin House.*

ANDREJ BLATNIK, *You Do Understand.*
Law of Desire.

LOUIS PAUL BOON, *Chapel Road.*
My Little War.
Summer in Termuren.

ROGER BOYLAN, *Killoyle.*

IGNÁCIO DE LOYOLA BRANDÃO, *Anonymous Celebrity.*
Zero.

BONNIE BREMSER, *Troia: Mexican Memoirs.*

CHRISTINE BROOKE-ROSE, *Amalgamemnon.*

BRIGID BROPHY, *In Transit.*
The Prancing Novelist.

GERALD L. BRUNS, *Modern Poetry and the Idea of Language.*

GABRIELLE BURTON, *Heartbreak Hotel.*

MICHEL BUTOR, *Degrees.*
Mobile.

G. CABRERA INFANTE, *Infante's Inferno.*
Three Trapped Tigers.

JULIETA CAMPOS, *The Fear of Losing Eurydice.*

ANNE CARSON, *Eros the Bittersweet.*

ORLY CASTEL-BLOOM, *Dolly City.*

LOUIS-FERDINAND CÉLINE, *North.*
Conversations with Professor Y.
London Bridge.

MARIE CHAIX, *The Laurels of Lake Constance.*

HUGO CHARTERIS, *The Tide Is Right.*

ERIC CHEVILLARD, *Demolishing Nisard.*
The Author and Me.

MARC CHOLODENKO, *Mordechai Schamz.*

JOSHUA COHEN, *Witz.*

EMILY HOLMES COLEMAN, *The Shutter of Snow.*

ERIC CHEVILLARD, *The Author and Me.*

ROBERT COOVER, *A Night at the Movies.*

STANLEY CRAWFORD, *Log of the S.S. The Mrs Unguentine.*
Some Instructions to My Wife.

RENÉ CREVEL, *Putting My Foot in It.*

RALPH CUSACK, *Cadenza.*

NICHOLAS DELBANCO, *Sherbrookes.*
The Count of Concord.

NIGEL DENNIS, *Cards of Identity.*

PETER DIMOCK, *A Short Rhetoric for Leaving the Family.*

ARIEL DORFMAN, *Konfidenz.*

COLEMAN DOWELL, *Island People.*
Too Much Flesh and Jabez.

ARKADII DRAGOMOSHCHENKO, *Dust.*

RIKKI DUCORNET, *Phosphor in Dreamland.*
The Complete Butcher's Tales.

RIKKI DUCORNET (cont.), *The Jade Cabinet.*
The Fountains of Neptune.

WILLIAM EASTLAKE, *The Bamboo Bed.*
Castle Keep.
Lyric of the Circle Heart.

JEAN ECHENOZ, *Chopin's Move.*

STANLEY ELKIN, *A Bad Man.*
Criers and Kibitzers, Kibitzers and Criers.
The Dick Gibson Show.
The Franchiser.
The Living End.
Mrs. Ted Bliss.

FRANÇOIS EMMANUEL, *Invitation to a Voyage.*

PAUL EMOND, *The Dance of a Sham.*

SALVADOR ESPRIU, *Ariadne in the Grotesque Labyrinth.*

LESLIE A. FIEDLER, *Love and Death in the American Novel.*

JUAN FILLOY, *Op Oloop.*

ANDY FITCH, *Pop Poetics.*

GUSTAVE FLAUBERT, *Bouvard and Pécuchet.*

KASS FLEISHER, *Talking out of School.*

JON FOSSE, *Aliss at the Fire.*
Melancholy.

FORD MADOX FORD, *The March of Literature.*

MAX FRISCH, *I'm Not Stiller.*
Man in the Holocene.

CARLOS FUENTES, *Christopher Unborn.*
Distant Relations.
Terra Nostra.
Where the Air Is Clear.

TAKEHIKO FUKUNAGA, *Flowers of Grass.*

WILLIAM GADDIS, JR., *The Recognitions.*

JANICE GALLOWAY, *Foreign Parts.*
The Trick Is to Keep Breathing.

WILLIAM H. GASS, *Life Sentences.*
The Tunnel.
The World Within the Word.
Willie Masters' Lonesome Wife.

GÉRARD GAVARRY, *Hoppla! 1 2 3.*

ETIENNE GILSON, *The Arts of the Beautiful.*
Forms and Substances in the Arts.

C. S. GISCOMBE, *Giscome Road.*
Here.

DOUGLAS GLOVER, *Bad News of the Heart.*

WITOLD GOMBROWICZ, *A Kind of Testament.*

PAULO EMÍLIO SALES GOMES, *P's Three Women.*

GEORGI GOSPODINOV, *Natural Novel.*

JUAN GOYTISOLO, *Count Julian.*
Juan the Landless.
Makbara.
Marks of Identity.

HENRY GREEN, *Blindness.*
Concluding.
Doting.
Nothing.

JACK GREEN, *Fire the Bastards!*

JIŘÍ GRUŠA, *The Questionnaire.*

MELA HARTWIG, *Am I a Redundant Human Being?*

JOHN HAWKES, *The Passion Artist.*
Whistlejacket.

ELIZABETH HEIGHWAY, ED., *Contemporary Georgian Fiction.*

AIDAN HIGGINS, *Balcony of Europe.*
Blind Man's Bluff.
Bornholm Night-Ferry.
Langrishe, Go Down.
Scenes from a Receding Past.

KEIZO HINO, *Isle of Dreams.*

KAZUSHI HOSAKA, *Plainsong.*

ALDOUS HUXLEY, *Antic Hay.*
Point Counter Point.
Those Barren Leaves.
Time Must Have a Stop.

NAOYUKI II, *The Shadow of a Blue Cat.*

DRAGO JANČAR, *The Tree with No Name.*

MIKHEIL JAVAKHISHVILI, *Kvachi.*

GERT JONKE, *The Distant Sound.*
Homage to Czerny.
The System of Vienna.

JACQUES JOUET, *Mountain R.*
Savage.
Upstaged.
MIEKO KANAI, *The Word Book.*
YORAM KANIUK, *Life on Sandpaper.*
ZURAB KARUMIDZE, *Dagny.*
JOHN KELLY, *From Out of the City.*
HUGH KENNER, *Flaubert, Joyce and Beckett: The Stoic Comedians.*
Joyce's Voices.
DANILO KIŠ, *The Attic.*
The Lute and the Scars.
Psalm 44.
A Tomb for Boris Davidovich.
ANITA KONKKA, *A Fool's Paradise.*
GEORGE KONRÁD, *The City Builder.*
TADEUSZ KONWICKI, *A Minor Apocalypse.*
The Polish Complex.
ANNA KORDZAIA-SAMADASHVILI, *Me, Margarita.*
MENIS KOUMANDAREAS, *Koula.*
ELAINE KRAF, *The Princess of 72nd Street.*
JIM KRUSOE, *Iceland.*
AYSE KULIN, *Farewell: A Mansion in Occupied Istanbul.*
EMILIO LASCANO TEGUI, *On Elegance While Sleeping.*
ERIC LAURRENT, *Do Not Touch.*
VIOLETTE LEDUC, *La Bâtarde.*
EDOUARD LEVÉ, *Autoportrait.*
Newspaper.
Suicide.
Works.
MARIO LEVI, *Istanbul Was a Fairy Tale.*
DEBORAH LEVY, *Billy and Girl.*
JOSÉ LEZAMA LIMA, *Paradiso.*
ROSA LIKSOM, *Dark Paradise.*
OSMAN LINS, *Avalovara.*
The Queen of the Prisons of Greece.
FLORIAN LIPUŠ, *The Errors of Young Tjaž.*
GORDON LISH, *Peru.*
ALF MACLOCHLAINN, *Out of Focus.*
Past Habitual.
The Corpus in the Library.
RON LOEWINSOHN, *Magnetic Field(s).*
YURI LOTMAN, *Non-Memoirs.*
D. KEITH MANO, *Take Five.*
MINA LOY, *Stories and Essays of Mina Loy.*
MICHELINE AHARONIAN MARCOM, *A Brief History of Yes.*
The Mirror in the Well.
BEN MARCUS, *The Age of Wire and String.*
WALLACE MARKFIELD, *Teitlebaum's Window.*
DAVID MARKSON, *Reader's Block.*
Wittgenstein's Mistress.
CAROLE MASO, *AVA.*
HISAKI MATSUURA, *Triangle.*
LADISLAV MATEJKA & KRYSTYNA POMORSKA, EDS., *Readings in Russian Poetics: Formalist & Structuralist Views.*
HARRY MATHEWS, *Cigarettes.*
The Conversions.
The Human Country.
The Journalist.
My Life in CIA.
Singular Pleasures.
The Sinking of the Odradek.
Stadium.
Tlooth.
HISAKI MATSUURA, *Triangle.*
DONAL MCLAUGHLIN, *beheading the virgin mary, and other stories.*
JOSEPH MCELROY, *Night Soul and Other Stories.*
ABDELWAHAB MEDDEB, *Talismano.*
GERHARD MEIER, *Isle of the Dead.*
HERMAN MELVILLE, *The Confidence-Man.*
AMANDA MICHALOPOULOU, *I'd Like.*
STEVEN MILLHAUSER, *The Barnum Museum.*
In the Penny Arcade.
RALPH J. MILLS, JR., *Essays on Poetry.*
MOMUS, *The Book of Jokes.*
CHRISTINE MONTALBETTI, *The Origin of Man.*
Western.

NICHOLAS MOSLEY, *Accident.*
Assassins.
Catastrophe Practice.
A Garden of Trees.
Hopeful Monsters.
Imago Bird.
Inventing God.
Look at the Dark.
Metamorphosis.
Natalie Natalia.
Serpent.

WARREN MOTTE, *Fables of the Novel: French Fiction since 1990.*
Fiction Now: The French Novel in the 21st Century.
Mirror Gazing.
Oulipo: A Primer of Potential Literature.

GERALD MURNANE, *Barley Patch.*
Inland.

YVES NAVARRE, *Our Share of Time.*
Sweet Tooth.

DOROTHY NELSON, *In Night's City.*
Tar and Feathers.

ESHKOL NEVO, *Homesick.*

WILFRIDO D. NOLLEDO, *But for the Lovers.*

BORIS A. NOVAK, *The Master of Insomnia.*

FLANN O'BRIEN, *At Swim-Two-Birds.*
The Best of Myles.
The Dalkey Archive.
The Hard Life.
The Poor Mouth.
The Third Policeman.

CLAUDE OLLIER, *The Mise-en-Scène.*
Wert and the Life Without End.

PATRIK OUŘEDNÍK, *Europeana.*
The Opportune Moment, 1855.

BORIS PAHOR, *Necropolis.*

FERNANDO DEL PASO, *News from the Empire.*
Palinuro of Mexico.

ROBERT PINGET, *The Inquisitory.*
Mahu or The Material.
Trio.

MANUEL PUIG, *Betrayed by Rita Hayworth.*
The Buenos Aires Affair.
Heartbreak Tango.

RAYMOND QUENEAU, *The Last Days.*
Odile.
Pierrot Mon Ami.
Saint Glinglin.

ANN QUIN, *Berg.*
Passages.
Three.
Tripticks.

ISHMAEL REED, *The Free-Lance Pallbearers.*
The Last Days of Louisiana Red.
Ishmael Reed: The Plays.
Juice!
The Terrible Threes.
The Terrible Twos.
Yellow Back Radio Broke-Down.

JASIA REICHARDT, *15 Journeys Warsaw to London.*

JOÃO UBALDO RIBEIRO, *House of the Fortunate Buddhas.*

JEAN RICARDOU, *Place Names.*

RAINER MARIA RILKE, *The Notebooks of Malte Laurids Brigge.*

JULIÁN RÍOS, *The House of Ulysses.*
Larva: A Midsummer Night's Babel.
Poundemonium.

ALAIN ROBBE-GRILLET, *Project for a Revolution in New York.*
A Sentimental Novel.

AUGUSTO ROA BASTOS, *I the Supreme.*

DANIËL ROBBERECHTS, *Arriving in Avignon.*

JEAN ROLIN, *The Explosion of the Radiator Hose.*

OLIVIER ROLIN, *Hotel Crystal.*

ALIX CLEO ROUBAUD, *Alix's Journal.*

JACQUES ROUBAUD, *The Form of a City Changes Faster, Alas, Than the Human Heart.*
The Great Fire of London.
Hortense in Exile.
Hortense Is Abducted.
Mathematics: The Plurality of Worlds of Lewis.
Some Thing Black.

RAYMOND ROUSSEL, *Impressions of Africa.*

VEDRANA RUDAN, *Night.*

PABLO M. RUIZ, *Four Cold Chapters on the Possibility of Literature.*

GERMAN SADULAEV, *The Maya Pill.*

TOMAŽ ŠALAMUN, *Soy Realidad.*

LYDIE SALVAYRE, *The Company of Ghosts.*
The Lecture.
The Power of Flies.

LUIS RAFAEL SÁNCHEZ, *Macho Camacho's Beat.*

SEVERO SARDUY, *Cobra & Maitreya.*

NATHALIE SARRAUTE, *Do You Hear Them?*
Martereau.
The Planetarium.

STIG SÆTERBAKKEN, *Siamese.*
Self-Control.
Through the Night.

ARNO SCHMIDT, *Collected Novellas.*
Collected Stories.
Nobodaddy's Children.
Two Novels.

ASAF SCHURR, *Motti.*

GAIL SCOTT, *My Paris.*

DAMION SEARLS, *What We Were Doing and Where We Were Going.*

JUNE AKERS SEESE, *Is This What Other Women Feel Too?*

BERNARD SHARE, *Inish.*
Transit.

VIKTOR SHKLOVSKY, *Bowstring.*
Literature and Cinematography.
Theory of Prose.
Third Factory.
Zoo, or Letters Not about Love.

PIERRE SINIAC, *The Collaborators.*

KJERSTI A. SKOMSVOLD, *The Faster I Walk, the Smaller I Am.*

JOSEF ŠKVORECKÝ, *The Engineer of Human Souls.*

GILBERT SORRENTINO, *Aberration of Starlight.*
Blue Pastoral.
Crystal Vision.
Imaginative Qualities of Actual Things.
Mulligan Stew. Red the Fiend.
Steelwork.
Under the Shadow.

MARKO SOSIČ, *Ballerina, Ballerina.*

ANDRZEJ STASIUK, *Dukla.*
Fado.

GERTRUDE STEIN, *The Making of Americans.*
A Novel of Thank You.

LARS SVENDSEN, *A Philosophy of Evil.*

PIOTR SZEWC, *Annihilation.*

GONÇALO M. TAVARES, *A Man: Klaus Klump.*
Jerusalem.
Learning to Pray in the Age of Technique.

LUCIAN DAN TEODOROVICI, *Our Circus Presents . . .*

NIKANOR TERATOLOGEN, *Assisted Living.*

STEFAN THEMERSON, *Hobson's Island.*
The Mystery of the Sardine.
Tom Harris.

TAEKO TOMIOKA, *Building Waves.*

JOHN TOOMEY, *Sleepwalker.*

DUMITRU TSEPENEAG, *Hotel Europa.*
The Necessary Marriage.
Pigeon Post.
Vain Art of the Fugue.

ESTHER TUSQUETS, *Stranded.*

DUBRAVKA UGRESIC, *Lend Me Your Character.*
Thank You for Not Reading.

TOR ULVEN, *Replacement.*

MATI UNT, *Brecht at Night.*
Diary of a Blood Donor.
Things in the Night.

ÁLVARO URIBE & OLIVIA SEARS, EDS., *Best of Contemporary Mexican Fiction.*

ELOY URROZ, *Friction.*
The Obstacles.

LUISA VALENZUELA, *Dark Desires and the Others.*
He Who Searches.

PAUL VERHAEGHEN, *Omega Minor.*

BORIS VIAN, *Heartsnatcher.*

LLORENÇ VILLALONGA, *The Dolls' Room.*

TOOMAS VINT, *An Unending Landscape.*

ORNELA VORPSI, *The Country Where No One Ever Dies.*

AUSTRYN WAINHOUSE, *Hedyphagetica.*

CURTIS WHITE, *America's Magic Mountain.*
The Idea of Home.
Memories of My Father Watching TV.
Requiem.

DIANE WILLIAMS,
Excitability: Selected Stories.
Romancer Erector.

DOUGLAS WOOLF, *Wall to Wall.*
Ya! & John-Juan.

JAY WRIGHT, *Polynomials and Pollen.*
The Presentable Art of Reading Absence.

PHILIP WYLIE, *Generation of Vipers.*

MARGUERITE YOUNG, *Angel in the Forest.*
Miss MacIntosh, My Darling.

REYOUNG, *Unbabbling.*

VLADO ŽABOT, *The Succubus.*

ZORAN ŽIVKOVIĆ , *Hidden Camera.*

LOUIS ZUKOFSKY, *Collected Fiction.*

VITOMIL ZUPAN, *Minuet for Guitar.*

SCOTT ZWIREN, *God Head.*

AND MORE . . .